"Racy, well-written erc
likeable heroine with toug
and an evocative African l

drowning

jassy de jong

ASTOR
+BLUE
EDITIONS

DROWNING
Astor + Blue Editions
Copyright © 2014 by Jassy De Jong

All rights reserved, including the right to reproduce this book or portions thereof, in any form under the International and Pan-American Copyright Conventions. Published in the United States by:

Astor + Blue Editions
New York, NY 10036
www.astorandblue.com

Publisher's Cataloging-In-Publication Data

DE JONG, JASSY. DROWNING.—1ˢᵗ ed.

ISBN: 978-1-938231-96-4 (paperback)
ISBN: 978-1-938231-97-1 (epdf)
ISBN: 978-1-938231-98-8 (epub)

1. Women's Erotica—Fiction. 2. American Photographer swept up in unexpected romance—Fiction 3. Contemporary Sex and Romance story—Fiction 4. High Adventure, in South African Bush Lodge—Fiction 5. Sex and Flirtation—Fiction 6. American Love story—Marriage and Infidelity 7. South Africa and New York City I. Title

Jacket Cover Design: Danielle Fiorella

For Dion, with all my love.

CHAPTER 1

I DON'T REMEMBER DROWNING.

I know it happened, of course, and I'm sure, locked away somewhere deep inside my mind, is the memory of what it was like. There are glimpses, now and again. The moment when the road began to collapse under the tires. How the floodwater streaming over the bridge stopped pushing against the car and started carrying it. The bobbing and bouncing as the little Toyota Yaris became suddenly unsteady, tumbling cork-like down the river before water began spurting inside.

It happened very fast. Perhaps I was screaming, shouting, struggling in panic. Or maybe I was paralyzed by shock while the car rocked and spun. I don't remember if my life flashed past me or not. I don't even know if I closed my eyes. If they were open, I would have been watching as the brown, foamy floods rushed in, covering me as it forced out the air, so that I was able to feel the water's cold kiss on my breasts, my neck, my lips…

I'd never been afraid of water until that day. I'd always loved it. I adored swimming, submerging myself in its cool, blue depths, becoming one with it. I reveled in the feel of my long, dark hair streaming out behind me, my body all but weightless, my pale limbs shimmering in pearlescent hues.

In fact, when my husband had asked me what my favorite sexual fantasy was, I'd answered that it would be making love in water.

We'd been in bed at the time, in his elegant Soho loft apartment. It was a few months earlier, soon after we'd come back from honeymoon. We'd had a fight the previous night and he'd gone to bed silent and angry. When I'd awoken the next morning to find his fingers tracing the curve of my breast, I'd shivered in delight at the intimacy of his touch, and knew I was forgiven.

"So," Vince had said, his voice soft, "what do you fantasize about sexually, Erin? Tell me. I want to know. Give me your favorite fantasy. Your wildest one."

The question had taken me by surprise. What could I think of? How could I impress Vince with my answer?

"My fantasy?" I'd repeated, playing for time, my brain muzzy from sleep and confusion and desire. His fingertips were circling my hardening nipple now. He pinched it gently and I gasped. "Let me think… It's… it's making love in water."

The minute I voiced it, I knew it was true. I pictured us in a clear lake somewhere, sun dancing on its surface. I imagined the flow of water against my naked skin as I waded toward him, wrapping my arms around his lean, toned body. He would smooth his hands down my back, caressing the curves of my buttocks as we kissed, his tongue sliding into my mouth. He'd hold me close to him, and as we moved out into the depths, our bodies would grow lighter, buoyed up by the lapping waves…

My thoughts had been interrupted by Vince's laugh.

"In water?" he'd asked. "That's not very original. I expected you to come up with something more imaginative that that, baby."

The warm friction of his tongue on my nipple had taken the sting from his words.

Almost.

"I was thinking of something really adventurous," he'd said. "Are you up for it?"

"Of course," I'd agreed quickly, hoping enthusiasm could make up for my own lack of imagination.

"Touch me while I tell you." He guided my hand down and I closed my fingers around his shaft, which was fully erect and felt warm to my grasp. I stroked him in the way he'd showed me he liked it while he whispered in my ear, "I want us to go to the couch on the balcony, and have a quickie there. It's getting light now, so there's the risk somebody might see. That's what makes it exciting. Shall we, Erin?"

Well, I could only hope none of the residents with a view of our sixteenth-floor balcony were early risers. It was difficult to say no to my husband, though; he usually got his way, as he did that time.

I still thought about my fantasy, though. Sometimes, I would dream about it. On waking, my mind would be filled with sensual coolness, the remembered softness of an intimate touch, the glimmer of sunlight on skin. And I hoped that one day, when we traveled out of the city to an exotic foreign location, it might happen.

At the time the accident occurred, I was on my way to Kruger Park in South Africa. Vince and I were driving in a convoy—well, by then, his rented Land Rover was a good few miles ahead. I was belted into the passenger seat of the Toyota while Bulewi, the driver, who must have been all of nineteen years old, clutched the steering wheel with tight fingers and peered anxiously through the rain-spattered windshield.

We had taken a wrong turn earlier in the afternoon and were now lost. We were driving down a dirt track so rugged and uneven it really didn't deserve to be called a road at all, in a storm so apocalyptic that it was like being inside a gigantic car wash. Sheets of water were being flung at the little Toyota from every direction. How Bulewi was seeing anything was a mystery to me, because in between the passes of the frantically moving wiper blades, I could find only a solid grayness.

Rain pounded on the car roof and the tires made a hissing sound as they cut through pooled water.

"Are you sure…" I began, convinced we'd left the track and were now driving through uncharted bushveld. I was afraid to tear my gaze away from where I hoped the road was for even a moment, but I needed to check that the carefully packed bags and boxes of camera equipment hadn't shifted from their positions in the back seat during this bumpy ride.

As I looked around, the car tilted sickeningly to the left, bludgeoned by a wall of moving water, and I heard Bulewi yell, "Shit!"

The rushing sound suddenly grew much louder and I was aware we were falling, spinning, and then...

Then nothing.

I have no memory of Bulewi fumbling to undo my seatbelt before escaping through his window into the cold, storming river. I recall only flashes of the gushing streams flooding inside, of the car growing heavier, becoming one with the body of water surrounding it. The level creeping upwards, covering my body, lapping at my face, trickling in between my parted lips and, as the car finally slipped under, submerging me completely so that my hair floated over my wide, sightless eyes.

Out of the blackness that followed, I surfaced into a vivid dream where Vince was making love to me by the side of a lake. His body pounded into mine with powerful, rhythmic strokes. His arms were enfolding me tightly; holding me so close that he crushed the air out of me. In his passion, his lips were bruising my own. I was overwhelmed by his presence, his strength.

"Don't leave me," he shouted. "Don't leave me! I'm not going to lose you!"

I wanted to tell him that he was never going to lose me, but I saw that the lake was rising, starting to engulf us. I feared that the waters would feel cold, but when they covered me, they were warm as blood. I reached for Vince, but could not find him. I understood suddenly that he had never been there at all; that I had been ravished by a stranger. Panicked, I cried out for my husband, willing myself to wake from this nightmare, but I could not rouse myself, and in my dream, I realized he was gone.

☩ ☩ ☩

When I opened my eyes again, I was lying on my back and looking up into a roaring darkness.

My first thought: My head was aching, my throat was sore, and it hurt to breathe.

My second thought: I had no idea where the hell I was or how on earth I had gotten here. I was utterly disoriented.

I tried to sit up, an action that did little to improve my situation. My head spun as I propped myself on my right elbow, and a tube that was attached to my face by a piece of adhesive tape tugged painfully.

Vince. Where was he? What the hell was going on here?

"Help!" I shouted. Well, I tried to, but it came out as a hoarse, unrecognizable croak. Why was this tube here? I lifted my hand to feel. Cool air was filtering through it into my nostrils. Oxygen, I guessed.

And then a beam of light cut the darkness, pinning me in its glare, and a warm hand closed firmly over my left one.

"Easy," a man's voice said, the tone calm but authoritative. "Take it easy. You'll feel better if you lie down again."

Who was speaking? I had no idea. I blinked, the bright assault temporarily blinding me and leaving purple dots and slashes on my vision.

My heart was hammering as I lowered myself back down onto my pillow. I tried to speak again. Still no luck. The flashlight beam moved away from my face and pointed upward onto what appeared to be a high, thatched ceiling.

The speaker let go of my hand, leaving me feeling oddly alone. Then the tape was quickly removed and the tube lifted away from my face. He cupped his hand behind my head and raised it gently. A glass touched my lips. Water. I gulped greedily.

"That oxygen tank's just about finished," he told me, lowering me back to the pillow again. "You should be fine without it now, but let me know if you feel short of breath, or if you have any chest pain."

"What happened to me?" I asked. Finally, success. I could speak again.

"You almost drowned."

The speaker's voice was deep and compelling. I couldn't place his accent, although I could have listened to his voice all day. Or, in my current circumstance, all night.

"Where am I?"

"At Leopard Rock Lodge, near Kruger Park."

Now I could recall the details of our trip. Boarding the plane at JFK, landing at O.R. Tambo in Johannesburg. Packing our gear into the Land Rover and driving out of the city, through miles and miles of farmland, and then deeper into countryside that had become progressively wilder and more beautiful.

"Why are the lights off?" I asked, wondering for a moment if this lodge was so remote that it didn't even have electricity.

"The power went down in the storm. I don't know why yet. There's an emergency generator here, but the lights aren't connected up to it."

The storm... new memories were beginning to surface. Panicked memories. The claustrophobic feel of being battered by tons of falling water. The slippery, squirming path of the car as it fought through liquid mud.

Cutting my gaze sideways I could see a darker shape against the darkness where he was, but that was all.

I moved my left hand and, sensing it perhaps, he grasped my hand again.

"Breathing all right?"

"I'm fine, thanks. Please tell me—where's Vince?" I tightened my fingers around his as I asked the question. He squeezed my hand back. His grasp was firm; his skin was smooth but not soft. His hand felt strong and capable, the same way his voice sounded. Its warmth was like a lifeline, holding me back from the darkness and confusion.

"Who's Vince?"

"My husband."

"He wasn't in the car with you." It was a statement, not a question.

"No, I... he..."

"Your driver said you were the only passenger."

"My driver! Bulewi. Is he okay?"

"Miraculously, yes. He got out of the car and managed to grab hold of a tree on the opposite side of the river, and climbed to safety just before the flood worsened. He said he tried to free you. He didn't manage, but he did undo your seatbelt, which could well have meant the difference between life and death when we reached you."

"Oh," I considered this for a while. "I'm so glad Bulewi is okay. Vince wasn't in the car with us. He was driving ahead, in the Land Rover."

"Then he would have got over the bridge. Your car was crossing just as it collapsed."

"So he's all right?"

"I assume so."

Relief filled me, but at the same time I couldn't help feeling a twinge of anxiety, knowing how angry Vince had been with me in the hours before the crash, and that it would be up to me to make things right between us.

"Can I call him?"

"The phone lines are down now. Hopefully they'll be back up tomorrow."

"What time is it?"

"About eight p.m."

I closed my eyes. I felt so tired, but at least the pain in my head was abating. A rapid drumming noise filled my ears. Rain on a high roof, the noise repetitive and strangely soothing. The storm hadn't stopped yet.

As I drifted into a dreamless sleep, comforted by the warm pressure of the stranger's fingers still touching my own, I couldn't help feeling a nagging certainty that there was something important missing. Something I'd forgotten about.

❖ ❖ ❖

When I woke again, it was daytime.

I sat up. Doing so was easier than it had been the previous night. A golden expanse of thatch stretched above me, and light filtered in from a large window to my right, which was covered by a white curtain. The light was muted, as if I was seeing it through a deep grey lens. The bed itself was palatial; on a scale with the room, and the floor was tiled with large, pale gold granite slabs that echoed the warmth of the thatch.

"My camera!" I said aloud.

Oh, Jesus, my photographic equipment had all been in the car. Close to fifty thousand dollars' worth of cameras, lenses, flashes, tripods, memory sticks. Packed so carefully on the back seat, together with the Mac Air book, my luggage, and my purse with cash, credit cards, and passport inside.

I started to get out of bed, my heart pounding—thankfully, my head was not keeping time with it this morning—but realized as I swung my feet to the floor that my legs were bare and streaked with dried mud.

I was wearing no underwear either. The only garment I had on was an oversized pale grey T-shirt, in a soft fabric, with the elegant logo of a leopard outlined in black on its front.

I heard a light tap on the door and hastily scrambled back under the covers.

"Come in," I called, rather self-consciously.

The door swung open. A cheerful, middle-aged black woman with braided hair, wearing a smart, green-trimmed khaki pinafore and carrying a small pile of folded clothing, walked in.

"Good morning," she said, offering me a wide smile. "I'm Miriam. How are you feeling today?" Her voice was lilting and musical, accented with the flavor of her native language.

"I... I'm fine, thanks."

She placed the pile of clothes on the ottoman at the foot of the bed. Outside, I saw the light was darkening again. Thunder growled and the rain began lashing at the window glass. Now I understood the reason for the odd, grey light. It was still storming outside. Why was it called sunny South Africa, I wondered, when it never seemed to stop raining here?

"Welcome to Leopard Rock Lodge," Miriam said, just as if I'd checked in like a paying guest.

"Is this a hotel?" A hotel with oxygen tanks in its store cupboard.

"It was originally planned to be. Now it is privately run." She smiled. "I have brought some clothes for you. Your underwear is dry now." She patted the pile. "But your jeans, not yet. If you look through here, you should find something that fits."

A hotel with oxygen tanks in its pantry *and* a selection of ladies' summer clothing?

"Thank you," I said.

"Mr. Nicholas said you should eat something, if you can. Breakfast will be served in half an hour, in the dining room down the passage. Or I can bring a tray to you in bed if you like."

Mr. Nicholas? I blinked at Miriam, wondering who he was. The man who'd held my hand last night? Then, as her words sank in, I realized that I was ravenous.

"I'll come to the dining room. And could I possibly use a phone? I need to make some urgent calls."

"I hope Mr. Nicholas can arrange it," she replied. It didn't sound like a very positive response. Perhaps the lines were still down, but in that case somebody must surely have a cell phone I could borrow.

Giving me another friendly smile, Miriam walked to the door and left the room, closing it gently behind her.

I planted my feet on the floor and stood up slowly. My long dark hair had dried in twisted clumps and I could feel grit in it, and on my scalp, as well as a few grains of sand in my mouth. Taking off the shirt, I found that moving and breathing were painful. My chest felt as if it had been pounded by a hammer and I had visible bruising on the inside of my left breast. From the seatbelt, perhaps? Surely not, if Bulewi had managed to undo it.

A khaki toiletry bag lay on top of the pile Miriam had brought. In it, I found a toothbrush and toothpaste, a small hairbrush, a mini shampoo and conditioner, and a travel pack that contained designer-brand body wash, scent, and skin care.

So, here I was, in what according to Miriam was an up-market lodge that was now in private hands. There was no phone in my room, I'd had my wet clothes removed while I was unconscious, and I was minus all my personal possessions, which were presumably somewhere at the bottom of a flooded river. A phone did not seem to be readily available, and I would have to await the mysterious Mr. Nicholas's pleasure if I wanted to make any calls. What was this place? *Hotel California?*

I could only hope that I would be able to call Vince first thing that morning to tell him where I was, and to stop the runaway train of disaster that had been set into motion yesterday.

CHAPTER 2

HALF AN HOUR LATER, I was showered, with my hair combed but still damp, because the outlet for the hairdryer was not working—more power saving, I supposed. I was dressed in my own freshly laundered underwear, a large T-shirt, and cotton shorts that were approximately my size. I put on a pair of oversized sandals and fastened the straps tightly.

Then I followed the delicious aroma of coffee down the wide, tiled passage, and into a huge dining room with enormous glass doors at the far end. Through them, I could see grey sheets of rain fading into dull green haze.

Several tables of varying sizes were set out in the room, but only one was covered with a starched white cloth. I took a seat on one of the comfortably cushioned wooden chairs just as Miriam appeared through a side door, carrying a jug of coffee.

She placed in front of me a large porcelain mug with an artistic rendition of a zebra on it before pouring.

"Hot or cold milk?" she asked.

"No milk, thanks."

Miriam topped up my coffee before asking, "Would you like scrambled eggs? Bacon? An omelet? Or we could do you a Continental meal. Toast, fruit, cheese, preserves?"

"I'd love some toast, and some cheese and fruit, thanks. Is there any way I could quickly speak to Mr. Nicholas?"

"Of course. He's outside, talking on the radio in the truck. Do you want me to tell him to come here when he's finished?"

"I'd better see him now, I think." After all, what if he was about to leave? I desperately needed to connect with reality, to sort out the disarray that was now my life. Call Vince and tell him I was okay. Contact the embassy to arrange a new passport, and the insurance company to report the loss of my equipment.

"Come this way."

My mind whirling with all the logistical issues, I followed her into a massive, airy kitchen with endless granite surfaces and two gleaming gas stoves, and then out into a scullery. She opened the back door, letting in the coolness of the rain.

A narrow covered walkway led to the side entrance of a large triple garage a few yards away. I edged my way up the covered walk, keeping close to the wall and doing my best to avoid the chilly, gusting downpour.

Parked inside the garage was the dirtiest Toyota Land Cruiser I had ever seen. Its white paintwork—well, I presumed it was white— was almost totally obscured by dried mud. The hubcaps were caked in the stuff, with occasional tufts of grass clinging to them. Great slashes of mud streaked up the vehicle's sides, covering the rear windows. The back of the car was a solid mass of dirt.

For a room that was home to such a filthy car, the garage itself was extremely neat. Only two broad, muddy tracks soiled its pristine floor. The strip light in the ceiling was on, although it made little difference in the general dark gloom of that rainy morning. I could hear the crackle of a radio coming from the car, and saw that the driver's door was open.

Stepping carefully to avoid the tracked mud, I made my way toward the open door, and as I did so I recognized the voice I'd heard the previous night.

"No. The road is totally impassable. Do you copy? The bridge has been washed away."

Strong, deep, authoritative, the words clipped but the accent impossible to place. Not quite British, but definitely not the local South African I'd heard spoken here. A blend of both, perhaps.

The radio crackled again, the speaker saying something I couldn't make out, and he replied, "We'll have to fly those down to them. Get a search and rescue operation under way as soon as the storm is over."

As I reached the open door, the man in the car turned his head and looked straight at me.

I was dazzled by the blaze of his light, extraordinary blue-green eyes. The palest turquoise, burning in the sculpted gold-tanned planes of his face. Blinking, I took in his strong bone structure, a trace of stubble along the firm line of his jaw. His tousled sandy-blonde hair looked to be in need of a cut, although for some reason its disarray only added to his attractiveness.

Under his faded blue T-shirt, his shoulders looked broad and powerful.

Mr. Nicholas was astoundingly good-looking, in an utterly masculine and somewhat rugged way. God, my camera would love him, if only it weren't at the bottom of a flooded river.

Briefly, I wondered how old he was. Crow's feet at the corners of his eyes suggested a certain maturity. Early thirties, perhaps?

How exactly had I landed myself in a luxury game lodge owned, or managed at least, by this demi-god? For a moment, I wondered if I was unconscious in the hospital somewhere and this was all an elaborate dream.

I wasn't dreaming, of course not. This was real. In fact, he was looking me up and down, too; his gaze traveling over me in a way that was both assessing and approving. I watched him take in my deep blue eyes and freshly washed dark hair, and saw that he noted how my borrowed shorts, too summery for this chilly rainstorm, exposed a fair amount of my legs, slender and still pale from the winter weather I'd left behind at home.

In his left hand he held the crackling radio receiver, and he lifted it to speak again into the mike, "I have to go. I'll be back in five. You copy? Over."

He put the radio down and turned back to me.

"You're looking a lot better this morning. How are you feeling?"

Reaching out, he took hold of my right hand, and I tensed for just a moment as he held it in his warm, firm grasp. The fingers of his other hand pressed on the inside of my wrist in a practiced manner. His touch was just the way I remembered it. I had never imagined, though, that the stranger sitting so patiently by my bedside in the darkness last night had been this man. That fact made me feel surprisingly short of breath. If I'd known… if I'd been able to see him, I don't know if I would have held his hand so innocently.

"I'm fine, thank you. Apart from feeling rather shaken up. And my chest is bruised."

"Pulse is a touch faster than normal," he observed, gently releasing my wrist. "Nothing to worry about, though. As far as the chest goes, I'm to blame for that. By the time I pulled you out, your lungs were flooded and your heart had stopped. I had to do CPR for a while before you came back."

I stared at him, looking into those piercing, unusual eyes as his gaze burned into mine. I couldn't help feeling astonished by what he had just said. My heart had stopped? My *heart*? No way. And he'd had to do CPR… I had a sudden vision of this man bent over me, pounding at my chest with the heels of his hands, crushing my lips with his own as he forced the life back into me. The image was shocking, but at the same time it made me feel strangely warm inside.

"Thank you," I said, in a rather shaky voice. "I had no idea… I didn't know my condition had been so serious."

"It was. I'm a trained paramedic, but even so I thought I'd lost you."

Suddenly, I wondered if his voice had been the one I'd heard in my dream; the mystery lover by the lake who had shouted 'Don't leave me!' Could that have been a fragmented memory from my resuscitation? I thought it likely, but felt too shy to ask.

Seeing that I was temporarily stumped for words, he said, "I haven't introduced myself. Nicholas de Lanoy."

"Erin Mitchell."

"Where are you from?"

"New York."

"Well, Erin, all I can say is you New Yorkers are made of tough stuff."

He put the radio receiver back in its bracket, and I stepped aside as he got out of the car and slammed the door.

"Is there anything you need right now?"

"Actually," I said, "I came to ask you if I could use a phone—it's urgent."

Walking with me back down the narrow covered corridor, Nicholas kept to my left, shielding me from the spraying rain.

"Unfortunately, the answer is no. All our cellular comms went down in the storm, and as I told you last night, the landlines aren't operational either. I only have one radio connection, which is a direct link to our local police station. I've already reported that you're here, so when your husband gets in touch with the police, he'll find out you're safe."

"Would I be able to get a ride to the police station?"

"Also not possible. The flood washed away the bridge, so the only road leading into this estate is now impassable. There are rough tracks going through the valley into the Kruger Park, but those lowlands are completely underwater now. So, Erin, you are my guest here until conditions change."

"But… oh, okay, then." If there was no way out, there was no way out. I'd just have to explain this to Vince in a way that didn't make him angry all over again. And I certainly wasn't going to let my husband know about Mr. de Lanoy. The way things were between us now, telling him that I was stranded on an estate belonging to such an attractive man would be completely foolhardy.

"There's a very well-stocked library and a gym," Nicholas said, guiding me to my seat in the dining room and pulling out my chair for me. "We have a freezer full of food, a vegetable and herb garden, fruit trees, and an excellent wine cellar. You'll be comfortable here for now, and I'll come and find you the minute we have cellular connectivity again."

"Thank you," I said, overcoming my confusion for long enough to finally remember my manners.

"It's my privilege to be able to offer hospitality to such an attractive visitor." He stared down at me and the hint of a smile creased his delicious mouth. I had the feeling that if he'd taken my pulse again at that moment he might have advised me to lie down immediately. But he didn't. He turned and strode out of the dining room to carry on his radio conversation with the police, leaving me alone with my coffee and, briefly, at a loss for words.

CHAPTER 3

THE STRESSES OF THE past twenty-four hours had been more draining than I'd thought. After breakfast, and despite the large mug of strong coffee, I could not keep my eyes open. Refusing Miriam's offer of a guided tour around the lodge, I stumbled back to my bedroom to find that another uniformed housekeeper had just finished making up my bed and was wheeling out a laundry cart containing the muddy, soiled bedding.

Mindful of my underwear shortage, I removed my bra and panties before climbing gratefully between the cool, crisp sheets. My eyelids felt leaden. The sound of the rain had abated to a soft hissing.

I hoped Vince had contacted the police by now, who would have informed him I was safe.

He would want to know where I was. Probably, the police would have told him that I was at Leopard Rock estate. They might even have mentioned Nicholas's name to him, which gave me a sick feeling inside and ruled out the easiest explanation, the one I'd been tempted to give my husband: that after being washed off the bridge, I had landed up in an all-female commune, or possibly even a nunnery.

Still, I could always emphasize to Vince that I had barely seen Mr. de Lanoy, that he'd been sorting out flood damage in another part of the estate and I had been cared for by his wife. That would be a workable explanation.

With that problem solved, my eyelids became too heavy for me to resist and I closed them. I would think of Vince now, as I fell asleep. Then, when we saw each other again, I could tell him I'd done so; that as I'd floated away I'd had him in my mind. His whipcord-lean body and sharp, angular cheekbones. His dark eyes and shiny dark hair, cut and styled to perfection. The way his lean-fingered hands looked as they cradled his camera. How, the first time we'd kissed, he'd stared deep into my eyes and then…

The blaze of pale blue eyes meeting mine and the warm touch of a strong hand keeping me from the darkness and my own confusion… the sense of a powerful, masculine presence by my side. Watching those sculpted lips as he'd spoken to me in that deep, compelling voice…

Hey—hang on a minute. I was supposed to be thinking about Vince here. How exactly had Nicholas de Lanoy managed to sneak into my mind instead? I tried to push him out but his presence wouldn't leave me, and in the end, I gave up the battle and drifted away with the memory of Nicholas's fingers on mine.

⚜ ⚜ ⚜

I surfaced from my sleep as if coming up through water, pushing my way through the tangled reeds and tendrils of my dreams, lingering in the sun-warmed shallows where my skin was caressed by its gentle touch. I stretched, feeling it lap over my breasts and flow under my thighs, lifting me, buoying me up…

"Erin. Erin?"

I blinked, the familiar deep gold of the voice pulling me back to reality even while I knew I was hearing it only in my dream.

Then I opened my eyes to hear knocking at the door.

"Come in," I mumbled.

The door opened and Miriam bustled inside.

"Good evening," she said.

Evening?

I sat up, staring at the dull gold light coming from beyond the pale curtain on the western window.

"I've slept all day. I'm so sorry," I told her. "I wanted to take you up on your kind offer to be shown around the lodge."

"Whenever you are ready," she said. "And now, Mr. Nicholas has said you should get up, so I have come to take you outside to the *lapa*. I will wait while you get dressed."

Giving me a cheerful smile, she retreated outside, closing the door gently behind her.

The *lapa*? What was a *lapa*?

I peeked quickly through the western window on my way to the bathroom. The setting sun blazed, red and intense, through the dissipating storm clouds. On the horizon I saw the craggy silhouette of a mountain flanked by rolling, bushy hills whose slopes looked somehow dark and forbidding in the fading light.

I dressed quickly, putting on my own jeans, and chose a long-sleeved, clingy black jersey top from my limited wardrobe in case it was cold. Who did these spare clothes belong to anyway, I wondered. More than likely, I decided, there was in fact a Mrs. Nicholas and I would meet her this evening.

I was feeling more like myself again. Clearly, my body had now recovered from the near-death experience, and my mind felt sharper, too.

With a spring in my step, I left the bedroom and followed Miriam to the lodge's front entrance. Low-wattage bulbs were set in torchiers at intervals along the walls, giving the place a medieval feel. The front door was an enormous, carved slab of wood and I wondered what kind of giant tree it had come from. Outside, the air felt astonishingly fresh and pure. It was cool, but not actually raining. More lights, at ground level, showed the way along a tiled path.

Ahead, I saw the flicker of a flame. The *lapa* turned out to be a paved open-air area with a high thatched roof supported by sturdy wooden poles and beams. A large fire was burning in a brazier, and on the other side of the *lapa*, Nicholas was tending another, smaller fire, this one under a barbecue grill.

Stone-topped surfaces along the left side held an array of glasses and drinks, a large bowl of salad, and loaves of crusty bread. Comfortable chairs were placed around a large oval wrought-iron table. Two of the seats were occupied by men I hadn't seen before, who were having an animated conversation over their beers.

"Good evening, Erin." Nicholas put down his tongs and walked over to me. I wondered for a surprised moment if he was going to take my pulse again, but instead he placed a hand lightly on the small of my back before leaning forward and brushing his lips against my cheek in greeting. He might have intended the gesture to be casual, but it didn't feel that way at all. It was as if he'd trailed fire across my skin. When he took his hand away from my back, I could still feel its heat there.

The thought suddenly occurred to me that Nicholas had already seen me naked. Yesterday, he must have undressed me, peeled off my sodden, muddy clothing, perhaps toweled my body dry before clothing me in the oversized T-shirt I'd been wearing when I'd awoken. Now I sensed that there was a strange, slightly uneasy intimacy with the man who'd saved my life.

"Good news first," Nicholas said. "Your husband has contacted the police and been notified you're safe. The not-so-good news is that we still have no cell phone signal here."

So Vince knew I was okay. Thank God he didn't have to worry about me anymore. Although that meant he also knew I was here. If he'd seen the way Nicholas had greeted me… well, we would be heading for another explosive argument, for sure. But luckily he hadn't, and inside, I felt the blend of relief and trepidation that I realized I'd become accustomed to over the past few months in my recent marriage to Vince.

"Let me introduce you to Joshua and Nelson," Nicholas said, turning to the two men. "Joshua Mkholo is Miriam's husband, and he heads up the team who looks after this estate. Nelson Ntshweng is our grounds manager."

Rising from his chair, Joshua greeted me warmly, his teeth flashing in his dark-skinned face, and gave me a handshake I didn't understand, where the grip changed three times from a normal handshake, to an "arm wrestling" angle, and back again.

"The African handshake," he explained, beaming. "Here in South Africa, it is our traditional way of greeting. Pleased to meet you, Erin."

"Pleased to meet you," I responded. By the time Nelson shook my hand I managed to get the handshake right—at least, I hoped so.

"Joshua and Nelson are both fans of the *Orlando Pirates* soccer team. They are playing an important match later on, so you won't get a word in edgeways tonight. I haven't been able to so far," Nicholas joked, as the two men resumed their animated conversation. "Something to drink? Water? Fresh orange? Wine?"

"I'd love a glass of white wine." He was drinking red. He poured me a glass of *sauvignon blanc* so crisp and aromatic that it practically danced on the tongue.

"I really appreciate your hospitality," I told him, taking a seat next to him and near the pleasant warmth of the brazier.

"It's my pleasure."

"And I'm very grateful you rescued me."

"You were lucky. Joshua spotted the other vehicle crossing about twenty minutes earlier—that would have been your husband's, I suppose. Joshua drove straight back to the lodge and told me the river was beginning to flood the bridge. We were actually on our way down when we saw your car go over."

"My life didn't flash before my eyes," I told him. I took a sip of wine and added, jokingly, "Do you think I did something wrong?"

It was the first time I'd seen Nicholas laugh. His teeth gleamed white in his tanned face, giving him a rakishly attractive air, and his pale eyes sparkled. Laughing along with him, I couldn't help feeling a thrill of pleasure at having been able to tickle his humor.

"I don't know, Erin, but I certainly wouldn't advise giving it another try. Getting to that car took years off our lives." As he stretched forward to put his wineglass down, his sleeve rode back and I noticed for the first time a deep, ugly graze on his left bicep, the area surrounded by bruising.

"I was wondering about this lodge. It looks like a very luxurious hotel, apart from the fact I seem to be the only guest. But Miriam told me it is privately owned."

"That's right." Standing up, he used tongs to test the smoldering coals, sending a shower of sparks into the air, before placing meat on the grill. "It was originally designed as an upmarket guest lodge. The previous owners intended it to be a safari destination where international tourists could pay to hunt the big five—lion, leopard, rhinoceros, buffalo, and elephant—in an enclosed area. Canned hunting, they call it."

He turned toward me and, lit by the flickering flames from the brazier, his face showed his disgust. "Unfortunately—or rather, fortunately, they ran out of money soon after going into business. I bought it, but I've never used it for its intended purpose."

"Neither guests nor hunting?"

He offered a wry smile. "Neither of the two. The estate itself is in two parts. The inner section where we are now, which is fully fenced, covers about eight hundred acres. I've removed the predators from this area, which now contains limited game. Some zebra, warthogs and various antelope, as well as six black rhino; the only one of the Big Five I've allowed in here."

"And the other part?"

"The outer section is ten times that in size, and it actually flanks the Kruger Park itself. That border isn't fenced, although the roads are closed to tourists, so the big game, the elephant, the leopards, all the predators, can come and go as they please between the park and here."

"Oh, wow," I gasped, and was then struck again by the unfairness of having ended up in this wildlife Mecca with all my camera equipment lost in the raging river.

"Tell me, how did you get onto that flooded road in the first place?" he asked, as if reading my mind. "There's a far better tar road ten miles to the west of here, which is where most visitors go."

"Vince chose this route," I told him. "He thought it would be more direct, and there might be photo opportunities along the way. The weather changed all that, of course. We weren't supposed to take the bridge at all, but Vince made a wrong turn and we spent an hour getting lost before retracing our route."

"These back roads are tricky, even with the help of a GPS," Nicholas agreed. "You mentioned photos. So who's the photographer?"

"We both are," I told him. "My husband's the famous one, though."

"Is he now?"

"Yes. Vince Mitchell. You've probably heard of him. He's an award-winning fashion, celebrity, and advertising photographer." I could see Nicholas didn't know about him. He shook his head, smiling quizzically, which left me feeling slightly embarrassed. At any rate, everyone in photography circles had heard of Vince. He was the rock star of commercial photography, and, although still in his twenties, had already made an international name for himself. In fact, the reason why we were traveling to Kruger Park was because Vince had been commissioned to do a fashion shoot, which would appear in the March issue of *Vogue*.

"I'm still trying to make a name for myself," I continued. "Although I won't have much luck on this trip, since all my equipment was in the car."

"That's a blow. It's insured at least, I hope?"

"It is, yes." I couldn't help wondering, though, what the insurance company would make of the accident. I had no way of contacting them. I couldn't even send them pictures of the car, or any proof of the accident, since I had no idea where the Yaris was now. I had a feeling this was going to turn into a logistical nightmare.

Flames leaped from the coals, licking at the sizzling fat that dripped from the sausages Nicholas was cooking and sending a delicious aroma wafting my way. Swiftly, he moved them to the side of the grill and waited until the flames had died down before placing a number of thick, juicy-looking game steaks in the center.

"And have you been married long?" Nicholas asked.

"Just three months." Following a whirlwind courtship which had been almost as short. Sometimes I felt as if the past six months had been a dream. In May this year I had attended the Vince Mitchell exhibition at a gallery in Chelsea where, for the very first time, I had met my husband-to-be. Watching Vince speak about his craft, surrounded by the framed images of his latest collection, I'd been more than impressed by the looks of the lean, dark-haired, trendily dressed artist, and blown away by how he articulated his passion and vision.

Afterward, when the crowd of fans surrounding him had finally thinned, I'd shyly approached him to ask some questions about his work. He'd looked me up and down with his deep, intense eyes and had pressed his lips together, giving a small nod before replying.

"Come on," he'd said. "Let's go talk about this over a whisky."

To my amazement, I'd found myself bundled into a cab together with Vince's publicist and the manager of the gallery, and we had headed off to a trendy club in Tribeca. Three hours and about five drinks later, the manager and publicist had left and we'd started dancing crotch to crotch on the crowded floor, where I had added "phenomenal mover" to the lengthening list of Vince's admirable qualities.

A short while after that, feeling like the luckiest girl in the world, I had been certain I'd found my soul mate. I'd gone back with him to his Soho loft apartment, where we'd had coffee and he'd shown me more of his work. He'd told me I had a classically beautiful face and perfect cheekbones and that he'd love to take photos of me in the nude sometime. And then, as dawn had broken, we'd gone to bed.

"You nervous?" Vince had asked, his wiry fingers easing my panties down over my thighs as he leaned forward to accept my kiss.

"No," I'd whispered, but it was not the truth. I'd done some reckless things in my past, but I'd never slept with anyone the first time I'd met them. This was unfamiliar territory for me, and I felt overawed by Vince's celebrity status. There was no way I could say no to him, but what if I didn't live up to his expectations? What if I became just another of his conquests?

His mouth met mine and the kiss quickly deepened. I forgot my fears, pressing myself against his toned body as I submitted to his sweet plundering.

"What turns you on?" I asked when we finally broke the kiss, my hand moving to his crotch and caressing the steely hardness I felt under his briefs. "Show me, Vince."

He'd smiled, pushing me down onto his wide bed. He propped himself on one arm for a moment to stare down at my now-naked body, and pushed a stray lock of hair away from my face.

"You're gorgeous, babe," he'd murmured. "Exquisite. You're gonna photograph like a dream."

Then his body covered my own, his muscles taut, his skin smooth.

"I'll show you what I want," he'd whispered, his lips brushing my ear…

Nicholas's response interrupted my thoughts.

"Three months? So tell me something else, Erin. Do you and your husband always travel in different vehicles when you go on holiday? Like the Royal Family?" he teased.

I gave a small shrug, staring at the crimson coals and blue-gold flames in the brazier and hoping I'd be able to fix what had gone wrong between Vince and me, and get our relationship back to the way it had been on that perfect, amazing spring night when we'd first met.

"No. Not always," I replied softly.

CHAPTER 4

THERE ENDED UP BEING eight of us for dinner, including Miriam, all seated around the table under the *lapa*. It was a merry gathering and to me, it felt like a celebration of life. Conversation and laughter flowed around the table as freely as the beer and wine, although Nicholas cautioned me that, given my brush with death the previous day, I should restrict myself to no more than two glasses of alcohol. The first glass went straight to my head, and as I sipped at the second while savoring the tasty food, I realized that I hadn't felt so relaxed and at ease for a long time.

When morning came, it would most likely bring the return of cell coverage and with that, my worries and obligations would once again descend. But this night somehow felt like a holiday. More than that... it felt like a gift.

I was thoroughly enjoying conversing with Nicholas. In response to his questions, I told him about my love of art, and he surprised me with his knowledge of the subject. It turned out that we shared a liking for surrealism, Salvador Dali, and spent a good half an hour discussing the geometric, modernist works of Escher.

To my relief, he didn't question me any further on my relationship with my husband—but nor was he very forthcoming about his own history. The closest I got to finding anything out about Nicholas was when I asked him if he'd studied art. He shrugged and said, "Not formally. But I've spent a lot of time on my own, with only books for company." Then he steered the topic away from himself again.

I couldn't help watching the way his pale eyes blazed when he spoke about a subject he loved, and I found myself a couple of times having to stop myself from putting a hand on his arm when we laughed together. As natural as the gesture would have been, I was still mindful about what had so recently gone wrong between Vince and me. I had to learn to behave in ways that didn't hurt or anger my husband—even when he was not present.

But, thinking of that, I couldn't help imagining how I would be reacting to Nicholas if things were different… if I were single… how readily the spark of excitement I felt in his presence would kindle into desire.

Mortified at the direction in which I was letting my mind wander, I suppressed the idea hastily, relieved nobody would ever be able to know my wicked thoughts. It must be the influence of the wine, I decided, and pushed my half-full second glass away.

A lull in the now-mellow conversation allowed me to appreciate the silence of this mysterious place. Apart from the occasional crackle of the dying fire, all I could hear in the stillness surrounding us was the trilling of crickets and cicadas.

"The sky's cleared at last," Nicholas said. "Erin, there's a platform a short way up the hill that's a great lookout point. Do you want to see the Southern Cross? It should just be visible by now."

"Oh, yes, please." I leaped to my feet, nearly tripping over the leg of my chair. Then, stepping with more caution, I walked carefully with him up the paved track.

We left the flickering lights of the *lapa* behind and followed the winding path up a steep, rocky hill. My too-big sandal caught on something I couldn't see, causing me to stumble.

"You okay?" Nicholas asked. In the darkness he reached for my hand and found it. His fingers closed around mine, his grasp firm. His touch sent a tendril of warmth through me. "Nearly there."

Another minute and we were standing on a small tiled platform surrounded by a waist-high wall. I rested my hands on it, the smoothly plastered surface cool against my palms, and looking up, I caught my breath at the brightness of the stars. The Milky Way was spread out above me in clear, dazzling detail.

"You can't see it now, but the ground slopes away on all sides from this lookout point," Nicholas said quietly. He was standing close behind me. "It's worth coming up here in the daytime. The view is magnificent.

I found I was acutely aware of his presence and thought I could feel the heat radiating from his body. I caught my breath as I felt his hands touch my shoulders. Gently, he turned me to the right.

"Those two stars there, the ones near the horizon."

"I see them."

"They are the pointer stars, Alpha and Beta Centauri." His breath tickled my hair. "Draw an imaginary line between them, and now follow that line upwards to those four stars. Those form the Southern Cross, and from there and the pointers it's easy to calculate due south." His warm palms smoothed sensually over my shoulders and I clutched the wall more tightly.

A sinful surge of heart-racing excitement dizzied me. I'd been slow to realize Nicholas's invitation up to this lonely lookout zone had little, if anything, to do with his desire to educate me on the placement of the southern constellations.

This was a seduction. I could sense it in my heartbeat, suddenly fast and strong. I could feel it in every prickling fiber of my body. Worse still, I found that raw desire was flooding through me; the feeling both powerful and primal. For a moment it washed all logical reasoning away. I stood, immobile, the pulsing heat in the pit of my belly as pleasurable as it was forbidden.

I could not respond to him... I could not let myself fall.

But nor could I move away.

As if sensing my dilemma, he spoke.

"Erin." His voice was like a caress. His fingers smoothed a stray wisp of hair away from my face before moving down, brushing so lightly over the throbbing tips of my nipples that if I had not sensed otherwise, I might have thought the gesture to be accidental. As it was, I caught my breath at the intense stab of pleasure that this brief touch offered. His fingers smoothed down my forearms to caress my hands.

"You are a beautiful, very desirable woman. I am intensely attracted to you. And, since we're both going to be together for another few days, maybe even a week, I would like to make a suggestion to you."

I swallowed. "From the context, it sounds more like it might be an indecent proposal," I said. My voice was slightly hoarse.

"Oh, yes. Nothing decent about what I have in mind." He sounded as if he was smiling. "Erin, I want to take you to bed. I want to satisfy you sexually. Lots of times, in lots of ways. To make you come, and watch while you do."

His body was pressed against mine now, steely and strong, but it was the explicitness of his words that left me suddenly without breath. His thumb rested on the two gold bands on my wedding finger.

"Nicholas, I'm…" My voice was unsteady.

"You're married, I know. I'm fine with that. In fact, it's what I prefer. You don't have to worry about me pursuing you, or trying to stay in touch afterwards, because I don't do that. What I'm proposing is just a few days of raw, lustful, passionate sex. We'll keep it as discreet as you want. Play according to your rules, both in bed and out of it. And then, when the bridge is mended, you go back across it, to your husband and your life, and this will remain our secret."

His words, spoken in that low, caressing voice, were hypnotic. It would be so easy… so tempting, to abandon my morals. I wouldn't even have to say yes to agree. I could sense he was waiting for any signal. The relaxing of my body against his. The upward pressure of my fingers, twining through his own. Any sign, however subtle, that I had succumbed to the powerful lust I felt for him. And, by doing so, offered tacit agreement to his audacious suggestion and to the shameful pleasures it promised.

Any signal, because I had done nothing yet.

I had done nothing yet.

And I could not. This was a test. Was I, a newly married woman, going to succumb so easily to the physical charms of another man— albeit one to whom I was intensely, viscerally attracted?

I'd never cheated on a partner in my life, not even when I was dating boyfriends. And now, after just three months of marriage to a man I believed to be my soul mate, I did not intend to start.

With a monumental effort, I stood straighter, squared my shoulders, slid my hands from under his even as he lifted his own away.

He stepped back, allowing me to turn and face him. The distance between us felt suddenly cold, and I wished for him near me again, but such thinking was far too dangerous.

"Thank you for the offer." My voice sounded small and husky. "I am going to refuse it."

"I understand," he murmured.

My head felt suddenly clearer, and my eyes had adapted to the almost full darkness. I could see the path, a pale, curving track snaking down the hill and past the *lapa* where the coals of the brazier still glowed, to the faraway twinkling lights of the lodge.

"I'll walk back on my own," I told him. "Good night, Nicholas."

"I'll follow you back to make sure you get there safely. Good night, Erin," he said in a more formal voice, as if we were suddenly strangers.

I set off on the path toward the lodge, going as fast as I could in case he was tempted to catch up with me and test my self-control a second time. Although he didn't speak a word to me, I heard his footsteps behind me the whole way. Ten minutes later, I arrived back at the lodge. He opened the front door for me and while he was closing it, I hurried down the corridor to my bedroom, still feeling breathless and shaken by the storm of emotion, which my host's shameless invitation had unleashed inside me.

CHAPTER 5

DRIFTING IN AND OUT of sleep the following morning, I relived the events of the previous night, which I was sure had also been part of my dreams. How Nicholas had greeted me, managing to turn a simple kiss on the cheek into a gesture that had felt decidedly unchaste. The way he'd smelled up close—musky and masculine, and how he'd laughed, his serious expression lightening up; the hard, chiseled angles of his face softening into a roguish appeal. I had watched his hands while he'd cooked, noticing they were square shaped, long fingered, capable looking but sensual, too.

I clamped my thighs together and pushed my face into the pillow, letting out a sharp breath as I remembered that single, exquisite moment when his fingers had moved down my body, just brushing the tips of my nipples, sending a bolt of sensation through my body that had been completely out of proportion to the lightness of that touch.

And the audaciousness of his proposal… offered in that deep, compelling voice.

Oh, God, what on earth would have happened if I'd said yes?

I slipped a hand down between my legs, remembering his breath, warm on my neck. Thinking about the words he'd said. How he'd wanted to pleasure me sexually. To make me come.

Well, he was doing it now… I gently stroked my clitoris, replaying those forbidden moments over and over again in my mind. I knew it was shameful and wrong to fantasize about this man's wicked offer, but the crawling sense of guilt I felt at doing so was only adding to the intensity of my pleasure. It had been a while since I'd made myself come—quite a long while. In fact, if I was going to be honest with myself, it had been far too long since I'd last climaxed with my husband. When we hadn't been fighting, Vince had been either too tired or too busy for anything but the quick, rough sex I'd discovered he preferred. Now I was suddenly desperate for the unhurried release of orgasm, even if it meant lusting over what might have been with another man.

I thought of Nicholas touching my breasts again—this time, his fingers lingering there, caressing… I rubbed a hand over them now, realizing my nipples were achingly hard. He had said I was desirable. Did he have any idea of the desire he had awoken in me? What might have happened next, out there under those bright southern stars? Imagine if he'd started pleasuring me right then, just slipped my shorts down and slid his hands up my thighs and…

I gasped, writhing against my moving fingers, my breath quickening. I was at the brink of orgasm when there was a rapid knocking at my door. Miriam called, "Ma'am. Ma'am, can I come in?"

I snatched my hand from between my now-moistened thighs. Wide-eyed, I sat bolt upright in the sunny room as adrenaline flooded through me. Then, realizing I'd gone to sleep in the nude, without even closing the blinds, I bounced down onto the mattress again and tugged the sheet over me.

"Yes," I said. "Come in." My face felt searing.

The door swung open and Miriam wheeled a trolley in.

"Good news, my dear. Our cell phone signal came back an hour ago. Mr. Nicholas told me to bring you this."

The trolley contained a new-looking HP laptop computer and power supply, an Internet plugin device, a basic Nokia cell phone with charger, a hardcover notebook, a pen and a pencil, and a tray with coffee and a large glass of freshly squeezed orange juice.

Miriam set about offloading the trolley's contents onto the large desk near the eastern window. The arousal I'd felt earlier was gone, thanks to Miriam's well-timed knock on the door. Now I couldn't believe I'd almost masturbated to orgasm thinking of Nicholas de Lanoy and his outrageous proposal.

When I thought about what Nicholas had suggested—and of how close I had come to saying yes—I found myself flushing with shame. What was wrong with me that I could even have considered such an offer? That single moment of weakness could have ruined my marriage forever. How would I be feeling now, waking up in tangled sheets to find Nicholas sleeping beside me, knowing that I'd done something that could never be undone?

How dare he have made such a suggestion. And how dare I have come close to saying yes, if only for one misguided moment. Now, in the brilliant light of a sunny morning, I felt both cheap and insulted.

"Please tell Mr. Nicholas thank you," I said. My voice sounded cool and self-possessed. It did not betray the anger that suddenly seethed inside me, directed both at him and at myself.

"I will do, my dear. If you are going to be busy, could I bring some breakfast to your room?"

"Thank you."

"Pancakes? A waffle? Fruit salad? Lemon muffin?"

If she kept tempting my appetite this way that new bridge would need to be triple-reinforced.

"Fruit salad sounds perfect," I told her and then, weakening, "Perhaps a waffle as well. I know I shouldn't, but…"

"Good. I will make it for you with maple syrup and ice cream. You are too thin, my dear. You need to eat, so you can go home feeling strong."

Looking pleased by my decision to stuff my face with fatty calories, she left. I got out of bed, dressed, and then began the task of setting up my mobile office on the elegant wooden desk.

I had gotten everything up and running, made a to-do list, plugged my phone into the charger, and was sourcing phone numbers when Miriam came back with the breakfast tray containing a fruit salad with strawberries, mango, melon, and kiwi fruit, and a crisp, delicious-looking waffle with a scoop of ice cream and maple syrup.

When she had gone and I knew I'd have some privacy for the next little while, it was time for me to make my first and most important call. I needed to phone my husband. To tell him that I was fine, and to try to apologize for what had happened between us before the accident.

⚜ ⚜ ⚜

It had been such a small thing, this time, and looking back on it, I felt so confused.

Vince and I had spent the day before the rainstorm exploring the museums and restored buildings in the historic gold mining town of Pilgrim's Rest. We'd stayed over at an exquisite boutique hotel run by a delightful and clearly devoted married couple—Kevin and Byron. It turned out that Byron had an interest in photography, too, and the four of us had ended up having cocktails together and conversing before dinner.

I'd noticed that Vince had seemed to withdraw from the conversation, but had assumed he'd simply been getting tired of talking shop, so in the end it was I alone who had walked through the hotel with the slender, dark-haired Byron, admiring his work, and of course exclaiming about the loveliness of his wedding photos, before we had been served a splendid three-course meal prepared by Kevin.

It had been a wonderful evening. I'd felt so happy, and so welcome in South Africa after talking, sharing, and laughing with these two like-minded people. Vince had remained quiet, but I had innocently assumed he'd been tired.

It was only when he'd announced abruptly, before coffee was served, that he was going to bed, that I had realized too late that he was angry. He'd gotten up without acknowledging me, offering our hosts a terse thanks, and an icy knot had tightened inside me, quickly dissolving the warmth that had been there.

Whatever his problem was, I knew from his demeanor that he was blaming me for it. Somehow, inadvertently, I had done something wrong.

The coffee had been excellent, but I found I'd stopped enjoying it. As soon as my cup was finished, pleading weariness after the long drive, I'd hugged Kevin and Byron goodnight and hurried to join Vince in our bedroom.

Vince had his back to me and when I'd tentatively stroked his lean, sinewy shoulder he had not responded, nor offered any sign he was awake, even though I knew from the tension I could feel in his body that he was.

I'd spent a virtually sleepless night, and in the morning, when I was feeling sick with exhaustion and dread, the fight had started.

"How could you do that?" Vince had snapped angrily.

"What are you talking about? Vince, I don't know what I did!" I blinked tears away, my stomach twisting with nervousness. Damn it all… why did he have to get into one of his moods now, of all times?

"That makes it even worse," he'd told me. He'd stared at me, his handsome, expressive face and dark eyes showing only the bitterest contempt. "That you don't realize."

"That. I. Don't. Realize. *What*?" I had snarled back at him, finally losing my temper, and the next moment I let out a shriek as Vince grabbed my upper arm hard, digging his fingers brutally into my skin as he'd yanked me toward him. In that moment, I could see he was so angry he didn't know how badly he was hurting me. I'd tried to grab hold of the bed frame to keep myself on my feet, but I hadn't managed, and I'd ended up stumbling sideways and smashing my hip agonizingly against a sturdy mahogany desk.

"You were flirting. Damn it, Erin, do you think only of yourself? How do you think I felt last night, sitting there like a fool and listening, watching, while you basically threw yourself at that guy? It was disgusting. Humiliating."

"But… but he's… he's gay," I stammered out. That was one of the reasons I'd felt so easy, so safe, interacting with Byron. I knew there were strict rules regarding other men. I'd learned the rules fast over the course of our whirlwind relationship. I understood now how to modify my behavior to avoid these problems, because I knew Vince could become illogically jealous at times. It was, unfortunately, the flip side of his artistic, talented personality—the deep creativity and the passion we shared for our work that had first drawn me to him, and him to me.

"How do you know they're gay? Both of them could be bisexual."

"In any case, I wasn't flirting. I was…" God, what could I say that wouldn't make things worse? I couldn't say I was acting normally or he'd never trust me again. "I was so excited about the photography. It just made me… more expressive than usual."

"So that's what expressive means to you, does it, Erin?" His grip tightened again, his fingers clawing agonizingly into the flesh of my arm.

My breathing was coming fast. This was a bad one. I could see it in the hardness of his eyes, the set of his mouth. I wished, I prayed, for the old Vince back, the one that I'd had yesterday, who'd felt like my twin, discussing our relationship as he'd sped along the rough terrain in the hired Land Rover. Who'd taken it all in his stride without losing his temper when the Land Rover's tow hitch had sheared off after the trailer had hit a deep pothole, damaging the trailer slightly but luckily not the contents.

Within a couple of hours, my dynamic husband had organized another car as well as a driver—Bulewi—to transport our excess luggage, as I had not obtained an international driver's license before coming out here. He'd said this was a more practical alternative than trying to find somewhere that could repair both the Land Rover and the trailer while we were out in the middle of nowhere.

Now, I wished for the resourceful, upbeat Vince that I loved to come back again and for this unfamiliar, jealous stranger to be gone. Preferably, before he made me scream from the pain of his grasp.

"Vince, I'm so sorry. You know I love you…" I began in a low, pleading voice, but although his grip finally loosened, I could see my efforts were too little, too late.

"I'm driving on my own today," he'd told me, his eyes narrowed. "I need some space to think about this, and decide what I should do. You can go in the other car."

"No, damn it!" I was boiling with frustration at the unfairness of all of this, but at the same time I was starting to second-guess myself. Perhaps I had behaved inappropriately. Perhaps I had not realized how hurtful my actions had been. I had never been married before, although Vince had. I was afraid of being the failure; the one who was unable to make things work with this complicated, talented man. Clearly, I needed to be less proud, to be big enough to apologize—to beg, if that was what it would take. "Please! Look, I'm sorry. I'm really, really sorry. We can talk it through…"

My mind was racing, desperately planning how I would come across as cool and distant to our two hosts when we bid them goodbye, how I would show Vince that I really did mean what I had said and that I was anxious not to let the same situation happen again. Maybe I could manage to leave the hotel without speaking to Byron at all. I hoped so.

He'd opened the windows and stared out at a sky that looked as grey and stormy as our relationship felt.

"I'm driving on my own today," Vince repeated.

⚜ ⚜ ⚜

Now, I felt sick with nerves as I dialed his cell number from memory, noticing as I did so that it was eight-thirty in the morning. I imagined the signal bouncing between satellites during the surprisingly long time it took to connect.

It rang three times before he answered.

"Vince Mitchell."

With the unfamiliar number I was phoning from, he didn't know it was me calling, of course. Even so, I couldn't help smiling at the sound of his voice: the rushed, impatient way he had of speaking, as if there was never going to be enough time on the planet for everything he needed to do.

"Vince, it's Erin."

"Hey, baby. Thank God you're okay. It's so good to hear you." His voice softened, warmed, and with a huge rush of relief I realized it was going to be all right. I had been a fool to even anticipate that this conversation might be difficult.

"It's so good to hear you, too."

"I was so worried for you. The police said your car actually washed off a bridge."

"It did."

"It was raining so hard, I don't even recall crossing a bridge."

"We were a long way behind you when it happened," I reassured him. "Nobody could have known it would collapse. It was very sudden."

"But you got out okay?"

"Yes, I did." Better to say nothing about the drowning, I decided. It might trigger further questioning on the subject of resuscitation. "I'm fine and so is Bulewi. He ended up on your side of the river."

"Bulewi? Who's he?" I could hear suspicion in his voice.

"The driver," I told him, laughing.

"Oh. I forgot his name. And the car?"

"I have no idea where it is."

"It's gone?" His voice was suddenly louder. "Jesus Christ, seriously?"

"Seriously. It's underwater somewhere, I suppose. I know there was some of your gear inside as well. Can you email me a list of what was there? I'm online again now."

"Well, you can do it from my hotel room later, can't you? Where are you now?"

I took a deep breath. "I'm at a game lodge called Leopard Rock. It's run by a local couple. Mrs. de Lanoy and her staff have been wonderful to me." I crossed my fingers behind my back as I spoke.

"Give me the coordinates, and I'll come pick you up. I assume the bridge is passable again by now?"

Clearly, the police had given Vince only the most basic information, which was a good thing for me, but his ignorance of my situation was a problem I hadn't expected.

"When the river flooded, it was completely washed away."

"So how can I get to you?"

"You can't, Vince. I'm stuck here until the bridge is rebuilt. It could take a few days, apparently."

There was another short pause.

"You're kidding me," he said. His voice was hard. "It can't take that long. There has to be another way."

"This *is* the middle of nowhere, remember. The bridge is gone, and the lowlands are underwater, which means the tracks that go through to Kruger Park are also impassable."

"What about a helicopter?"

I had heard Nicholas mentioning something about flying supplies somewhere. Carefully, I replied, "I'll ask Mrs. de Lanoy. But I don't think there's one on the property."

"You mean you haven't checked yet if there's a helicopter available?"

"No. I didn't think of doing that." My mouth felt dry.

He was silent again.

"This is all very convenient, Erin," he said in a cold voice that made my stomach twist.

"H-how do you mean?"

"I don't know myself. It just seems… strange. That the driver managed to get to the other side of the river, but you ended up somewhere that has no way out."

"Well, I am telling you the truth." On the defensive yet again, I realized with a sickening sense of finality. I could see how this conversation was going to go; the way so many others had done recently. *You're lying to me. No, I'm not. Yes, you are. No, I'm not.*

"We'll see about that, I suppose," he said, thankfully choosing to cut the argument short. "I'll call you later when I've compiled a list of the equipment."

"I'll speak to you then. I miss you, Vince."

I could hear the placatory tone in my own voice, the neediness in my words.

We disconnected and I let out a deep, frustrated sigh.

This wasn't right. This wasn't fair. Why did I have to walk such a tightrope to assuage his imaginary fears? It was crazy that, in order to try and prevent an upsurge of the jealousy I'd come to fear, I'd ended up telling my husband a lie that could easily come back to bite me.

With hands that felt suddenly cold, I did what I hadn't thought of doing until now, but should have done before I told Vince this story.

I Googled Leopard Rock.

CHAPTER 6

FOUR PAGES INTO THE Google search I thought I was safe, primarily because there was another Leopard Rock, an up-market housing complex, in a different part of South Africa. I could only find three references to the Leopard Rock game lodge where I was staying now.

Two of them were outdated links on tour company sites, leading to a web page for the hunting safaris that was no longer operational. The other was an article on the expansion of Kruger National Park, which mentioned that the border with the estate had now been opened.

No mention of Nicholas.

Not, at any rate, until I reached page five.

The piece was on the blog site of Angela Sands, a twenty-four year old Australian travel journalist, and it had been written in June of this year.

The guide book promised me that Leopard Rock Estate was a brand new safari lodge, but imagine my disappointment when I arrived at the gate to find it was no longer operating as a business and had been sold into private hands. Fortunately, the owner, handsome bachelor Nicholas de Lanoy, was on the premises, and agreed to show me round this beautiful estate. An offer of dinner led to a wonderful week of enjoying his hospitality and touring the area, including several trips into Kruger National Park itself, where I saw and photographed all the Big Five.

The area is astonishingly beautiful, with warm temperatures year-round, and although Leopard Rock's luxury accommodation cannot, sadly, be enjoyed by tourists, there are a few other estates in the area that cater to visitors and are rated four- and five-star...

I read the blog post twice. Then I looked at the photograph of Angela herself. She was blonde and beautiful, smiling broadly and confidently out from the screen. There was no doubt in my mind that she had been made the same offer by Nicholas, and unlike me, had taken him up on it.

I buried my head in my hands.

If Vince Googled the estate and read to page five, I was in serious trouble. The words "handsome bachelor" said it all, and that was before the writer had offered the not-so-subtle hint as to why she'd stayed for seven days after being invited to dinner.

And this was not beyond the bounds of possibility, because Vince had used Google in the past to check up on where I had been when I went out without him. Once, we'd ended up in a huge fight because I'd told him I was visiting Daryl Anders, one of my girlfriends. While I was out, he'd gone online and found the name Darrell Anders, who turned out to be an ex-football star who lived in the Upper West Side. Vince became certain I'd gone to see the football star and even after he'd finally given me the chance to explain, I don't think he believed me.

The ice cream had melted on my waffle. Though queasy, I forced myself to eat half of it, along with a few more pieces of fruit, so as not to disappoint Miriam. The sun was pouring in through the window and I had a feeling the day was going to be a scorcher.

To my consternation, I found the shower was not working. Only a trickle of water dripped from the tap before it dried up completely. I smoothed my damp hands over my hot skin, then chose a fresh T-shirt and a pair of cotton shorts from the borrowed clothes in my cupboard. Now, I couldn't help wondering with a sharp and illogical flicker of resentment whether any of them had belonged to Angela the Australian journalist, so confident and lovely and three years younger than me.

Gathering up my courage, I went to find Nicholas.

❄ ❄ ❄

The morning was awash with sunshine. It streamed into the lodge, spilling onto the warm, tiled floor, causing the polished furniture to glow and the cream-colored walls to seem light and bright.

Outside the front door, the sky was a cloudless, radiant blue. The air was completely still and already very warm. The white Land Cruiser, restored now to a state of sparkling cleanliness, was parked next to the left wing of the lodge, further down the curving driveway. Joshua was outside, with two of the estate staff, loading up some large jerry cans from what I supposed was a store room into the back of the vehicle.

"Morning, Erin," he called.

"Morning," I responded. "Do you know where Nicholas is?"

"He's just come back from a run." Shielding my eyes, I looked in the direction he was pointing. "He'll be down there now, I think."

I looked and, for the very first time in radiant daylight, I could see the breathtaking view of the estate. The tarred driveway stretched down between ranks of tall, slender trees that I couldn't identify. On either side of the driveway was an expanse of green lawn studded with fruit trees. Further out, the manicured lawn gave way to miles of bushveld; emerald tufts of coarse grass, gnarled-looking thorn bushes with twisted branches, and a long way down the hill, I could see dense overgrowth following the meandering curves of a stream or river.

I walked across the grass toward the swimming pool, which was under a tall avocado tree with broad, dark leaves. Half the water was shaded by the tree and the other half sparkled in the sun. I could see some ripe fruit hanging from the tree—full, rounded, deep green in color.

Nicholas was swimming laps. He was doing a fast and efficient crawl stroke. His powerful arms cut through the water, and where the sun touched his skin, it shone in burnished gold. Watching him, I felt a complex mix of emotions. Relief that I had resisted his charms yesterday. Regret—shameful as it was to admit—for the same reasons. What would our night together have been like if I had said yes?

I couldn't help but imagine what it would have been like to wake up beside Nicholas. How he might have smiled at me with sensual promise in his eyes before reaching for me again. I wondered if his skin would be as silken to the touch as the water made it look. How would his body feel if I smoothed my hands over his shoulders, down his muscular back…?

I jumped as the cell phone in my pocket started to ring, wrenching me back to reality, and not a moment too soon.

Vince was calling again. Hurriedly turning my gaze away from the water, I answered as fast as I could.

"Hey there."

"I've got that list of equipment." His voice was cold. I could only hope that if he'd been busy making the list, he hadn't had time to look up Leopard Rock online.

"Great. I can't write it down right now, so if you could email it as I asked you to, that will be best." I had told him to send it online, so why was he calling? Since when was I his damned secretary?

I was surprised by the sudden surge of defiance I felt.

"You can't write it down? Where are you?" he pressed.

"I'm outside." The harsh cawing of a bird flying overhead confirmed my words.

"Outside where? You were inside when I spoke to you ten minutes ago."

"And now I'm outside," I said patiently, though once again I was starting to seethe with frustration. It seemed that enforced separation didn't sit well at all with Vince, which was something I hadn't had the chance to discover about him. During our passionate courtship and our subsequent short marriage, we'd spent just about every waking moment together.

That was clearly how it needed to be once again. We'd been so happy during that time, without the outside world intruding.

"Have you asked about the helicopter?" he said, his voice sharp.

"No, I haven't. It's only been a few minutes since we last spoke. I'm not Superwoman, you know. If I was, I could fly across the damned river." I was tired of his badgering, and if my words came across as sarcastic, I found I didn't care. My gaze strayed back to the swimming pool where I found myself mesmerized by the rhythmic stretch and flex of Nicholas's muscular arms.

"What are you hiding from me, Erin?" Vince asked, his voice surprisingly soft.

There was a long silence, during which I had the opportunity to regret my outburst.

"Hiding? From you?" I asked incredulously, managing to suppress a pang of guilt. "Nothing. I'm hiding nothing. This is how things are."

"Is that so?"

"Vince, look. I don't understand you. Why are you being like this? I'm the one who was in an accident. I'm the one who—who could have drowned when my car got washed off the bridge. If you don't believe me I'll—I'll go down to the bridge and take a photo of it later, on this phone."

"You do that," he said, cynicism dripping from the words.

"I have to go now. I'm going to find out about the helicopter."

"Let me know when you've done that, too," he said in measured tones.

"I'll call you back." I stabbed the disconnect button, furious at being so distrusted and disbelieved. More than that, I was disturbed by the fact that the man I'd married was starting to show such a different side. It left me feeling upset and vulnerable and very far removed from the cheery, unflappable Erin I'd always thought myself to be.

Turning once again to the pool, I saw Nicholas had finished his laps and was standing in the shallow end. I realized with a little skip of my heart that he'd been watching me, but as soon as he noticed me looking at him, he dropped his gaze.

I hadn't seen him in swimming trunks before and couldn't help but notice the tanned perfection of his rugged body, his skin glowing bronze in the punishingly hot sun. Gleaming with water, his muscles looked taut, ripped, hard as marble. Once again, I felt assailed by conflicting emotions. What was done was done. I had remained faithful to Vince. I had refused Nicholas's offer. But staring wasn't a crime... was it?

"Want a swim?" he called.

Did I ever!

"We switched off the pump this morning to save fuel, so there's no water in the rooms yet. Come on in. I'm about to get out."

To my relief, his voice was the way he'd sounded when we had first met. Firm, authoritative, with no trace of the intimacy I'd heard the previous night.

"I don't have a swimsuit," I said.

A slight smile warmed his face at those words. When it faded, I saw he was watching me again, more intently, the way a leopard might eye out its prey.

"Swim as you are. Your clothes will dry fast enough in this heat. There's a towel on the table under the covered balcony."

I put my phone down on the towel. Then I stood in the shade by the shallow end and dipped a toe into the water, which felt refreshingly cool, but not cold.

I sat on the tiles and looked at the lapping waves, catching a glimpse of Nicholas's sculpted legs as he strode away to get his own towel.

All I had to do was put my feet in. Then the rest of me. It wasn't difficult, so why did it suddenly feel as if it was? I loved swimming, so why was I finding it such a problem to get in? Looking at the expanse of water in front of me, I felt frightened.

"I think I'm okay, actually," I heard myself confess in a shaky voice.

There was a long pause. To my surprise, Nicholas discarded his towel and jogged back toward the deep end of the pool. He cut through the water in a clean, athletic dive and surfaced a few seconds later, shaking water from his tawny blond hair.

He swam toward me and waded the last few steps into the shallows. As he came closer, I could see droplets sparkling on his broad shoulders.

"You nearly drowned," he said. His pale eyes met mine, his gaze hypnotic. "It's not surprising you don't want to get into water again."

He held out his hand.

I took it.

"Don't be scared. There's no need to be," he said.

I'd been wrong to think that my "no" of last night had changed everything. The tension I'd sensed between us was still there; an attraction hummed like an electric current, growing more powerful the closer we got.

My legs slid into the pool, looking smooth and pale under the surface, slender in comparison to his muscular thighs. I could feel my clothing start to float around me and the cool touch of the water on my skin. I held onto Nicholas tightly and he held me. His skin was slick and wet, and under it I could sense the raw virility in every movement of his body as he buoyed me along.

"You'll be okay," he told me.

Slowly, he walked backward into the deeper water until it covered my breasts, my hair swirling around me. My legs pressed against his as I floated in the dappled shade—I wanted to wrap them around him, but I didn't dare, because it would be for all the wrong reasons. I could feel him breathing fast. His arm was around my waist; my hands were clasped over his shoulders.

Behind me, barely audible over the lapping water, I could hear the soft trill of my ringing phone.

Vince doesn't trust me, I thought, in a brief and illuminating moment of despair. *I'm already damned in his eyes, whatever I do.*

Nicholas and I moved toward each other in the same moment. My mouth brushed his, softening under his touch and then parting, opening. His lips were cool, but his tongue was warm as it slid against mine in an utterly sensual caress.

As our kiss deepened, I heard him groan with pleasure. The sound struck a chord of desire within me, causing my fingers to dig into his shoulders and him to pull me closer, holding me tight against him, feeling the firmness of his well-muscled body and the more intimate hardness of his arousal. I thrust my hips against it, feeling its thickness, the outward physical embodiment of the same desire that had pooled inside me.

The water might as well have been air or fire... I was no longer aware of it. I was aware only of the incredible, erotic dialogue of our lips and tongues. The hungriness with which he was kissing me—his actions so sensitive, surprisingly gentle and yet utterly masterful. It was as if he could read every thought I'd ever had about how I wanted to be touched. I could sense he was holding nothing back, and it was stoking a need deep inside me; an aching want begging to be fulfilled.

"Erin," he whispered, as we broke the kiss, both breathing roughly, my own astonishment at the intensity of what had just happened reflected in his eyes. "Jesus, Erin..."

He stared down at me, his lips parted.

Enough now. Enough—no more. I should say no, but I could not, as we were magnetically drawn toward each other again.

And then a rather deliberate throat-clearing caused us both to freeze, and to jerk our heads guiltily round in the direction of the sound.

Joshua stood a few yards away from the swimming pool, his hands behind his back and his gaze fixed on a small, white-blossomed bush that was nowhere near the pool at all.

"Er—Mr. Nicholas, the car is loaded up."

"Thanks, Joshua. I'll be there in ten minutes."

He turned back to me. His gaze devoured me. Holding me tightly, he paced slowly back into the shallow water before releasing me.

"Come with me," he said, and looking at the urgent need in his eyes, I knew this was not a question, but a command.

CHAPTER 7

I SNAPPED OFF MY phone before hurrying back to my room to change into dry clothes. As I did so, I noticed that Vince had already called again twice. I didn't know what to make of any of this. My head was throbbing with confusion, but other parts of me were throbbing for entirely different reasons.

That single, forbidden kiss... I had never experienced anything so electric, so erotic, in my life.

But what I had done was wrong, so very wrong. I had no way of justifying my behavior, other than that, in a moment of frustration and tiredness of defending myself from my husband's unfounded accusations, I had deliberately chosen to give in to temptation.

I was a weaker person than I'd thought, and I knew that I'd soon be paying for my actions with the heavy coin of guilt. I hoped that the drive with Nicholas would allow me to straighten things out between us. I just wished I wasn't feeling such breathless anticipation at the thought of being in his presence again.

My only set of underwear was now dripping wet, so I hung it up in the bathroom. Wherever we were going, I'd have to do without. I chose a close-fitting, lined tank top that would allow me to go braless and pulled a looser cotton shirt with elbow-length sleeves over it. My skin was cool and my small but well-formed breasts felt tight and aroused, my nipples responding instantly to the slightest touch.

I pulled on the other pair of shorts. I felt undressed without panties on. I wasn't used to going commando. I wasn't used to waking up in unfamiliar guest lodges after having nearly drowned, with none of my clothes or possessions with me. This situation was disorienting. The sooner I could get out of here, the better.

It was only one kiss. Just one—and I had been unreasonably provoked by my husband's paranoid behavior. One, surely, could be excused… as long as it did not happen again. It could not happen again.

"You've had your fun," I told myself sternly in the mirror, noting how flushed my face looked compared to its usual paleness. It had been a long time since I'd seen such color in my cheeks and lips and I thought it made me look lustful and wanton.

I took a deep breath.

"Pull yourself together, Erin," I warned my reflection. "When you climb into that car, you're going to explain to your host how this was all a mistake, and you're not going to play his games anymore."

The pool water had turned my long, dark hair from wavy to tangled. There was no time to comb it out properly, so I could do nothing more than rake my fingers painfully through it. My pupils were dilated and my mouth felt swollen with desire.

Telling myself that this impression was simply the product of a fevered imagination, I left the room and walked briskly through the lodge and outside, to where Nicholas was already waiting in the Land Cruiser, with the passenger door—on the left-hand side in South Africa—open for me.

"We're going down to my neighbors on this side of the river," Nicholas explained. "They called an hour ago to say they're running short of diesel for their generators. Which, for them, is critical because they own a game butchery and have five freezers full of meat right now."

I loved the deepness of his voice. The way he spoke—his accent. Those clipped British words with the hint of a South African flavor. I could have listened to him speak all day.

What surprised me, though, was his choice of subject matter. I'd expected him to be as unsettled as I was. But here he was, at ease in my company once again, conversing in a relaxed way about matters of interest.

"We'll definitely see some animals on the way," he said, as the mowed lawn transitioned to scrubby *bushveld*. "The zebra like to hang out on the borders of the forest at this time of the year.

"How many zebra do you have?"

"In this secure area, ten. Oh, make that eleven. There was a foal born last week. In fact, if we're lucky, we might... Yes. Look there. On the right. There's the herd, and there's the foal. A colt, Joshua thinks."

I peered in the direction he was pointing, narrowing my eyes against the bright sunshine, and suddenly the criss-crossed shade of the bushes translated itself into a dazzle of vivid stripes. The herd was walking quietly through the shadows, tails flicking, while the tiny new arrival capered, with surprising grace, at the heels of his mother.

"Oh, they're beautiful!"

I saw Nicholas smiling at my obvious delight.

"What are those animals beyond the zebra herd?" I peered through the scrubby bush.

"You've got sharp eyes. Those are two of our wildebeest, the animal that is the gnu. They've got nothing much going for them in terms of looks, as you can see. They're big and ugly and brown and hammer-headed." His voice was laced with humor.

"They're cute!" I protested.

"If you think so, then the term 'cute' coming from you is a terrible insult. I'll have to watch where you use it." He grinned at me. The expression was infectious and I found myself grinning back at him. Damn it all... I shouldn't be laughing with him now. I should be coldly ordering him not to flirt with me. How had he managed to disarm my defenses so completely?

Heading downhill, the vehicle jounced over a series of steep bumps in the road. Glancing up, I saw that the intense heat had already formed a series of cumulus clouds which bulked on the horizon, grey and threatening.

"We've got an hour, maybe two, before it rains again," he said. "Let's deliver this diesel. I'll show you the bridge on the way back."

⚜ ⚜ ⚜

When we arrived at the neighboring farm, I was introduced to the owners—Thandiwe, an elegantly dressed black woman, and her blonde-haired, German husband, Berndt.

"Thank you so much," Thandiwe said, as Berndt and Nicholas hefted the containers from the back of the truck and carried them into the garage. "We were planning to go into town as soon as the storm had passed. Bad luck about the bridge."

"Look on the bright side. At least you weren't stuck in town when it collapsed."

Nicholas's words were interrupted by a loud wailing. A chubby boy with enormous brown eyes and a halo of frizzy dark brown hair came running into the garage, blood spurting from a gash on his chin. He was followed closely by an anxious-faced girl a few years older.

"Mom!" she cried. "David fell and hurt himself in the garden."

Picking the boy up with concern in her eyes, Thandiwe turned—not to Berndt, but to Nicholas.

"Doctor," she said anxiously, "thank goodness you're here. It's all happening at once today. Would you mind taking a look?"

Nicholas examined the bleeding cut carefully.

"It should heal fine, but it'll need a stitch or two."

"Do you have your kit with you?"

"Always, Thandiwe."

I watched in surprise as he jogged back to the car, returning a minute later with a large plastic trunk. He pulled on gloves before removing the equipment he needed from the stock of supplies inside.

Berndt held the child on his knee while Thandiwe and I watched from a safe distance. The child's sobs abated as Nicholas spoke to him gently before injecting tiny amounts of what I supposed was a pain killer. Then, with precision and care, he closed the wound with three small stitches.

"I didn't know he was a doctor," I said to Thandiwe.

"Oh, he's not actually a doctor. We just call him that. He's a paramedic who's done years of work overseas. Or so he tells us." She smiled, looking at me with some curiosity. "He doesn't tell us much, actually. Are you—er—how do you know him?"

"He pulled me out of the river when my car washed away," I said. "I'm staying until the bridge is rebuilt."

Thandiwe clapped her hands over her mouth.

"No! You're the woman who almost died? Berndt took his tractor down to the river to help Nicholas reach you. He said it was the most frightening experience—a race against time with the car being washed downstream in that raging water. He came back and said Nicholas had told him your heart had stopped and he didn't know if you were going to make it."

"Well, so far, so good," I told her. "I'm very grateful to Nicholas. He's given me my life back." I added quickly, in a firm voice, "All the same, I can't wait to be home with my husband."

To my surprise, Thandiwe gave me a big hug. "I'm so glad you are okay."

With the stitching finished, Nicholas removed his gloves and packed his first aid kit away before washing his hands thoroughly in the farmhouse kitchen. Five minutes after that we were ready to go home. Before we left, Thandiwe thrust a large, heavy cooler bag into my hands.

"Here you go," she said, smiling. "As a thank-you."

"It's packed with meat, I'm sure," Nicholas said. "You didn't need to, Thandiwe. But it will be very welcome."

When we got into the car again, he asked me, "Do you want to go and see where the bridge was? It's just a little further down the road."

The early afternoon had become grey and cool, with threatening clouds bulking overhead.

"As long as you don't think we'll get washed away again," I said, looking nervously at the sky.

"No chance of that. It'll take a few hours of sustained downpour to cause another flood."

He started the car and we headed down the muddy sand road in the direction of the river.

"I don't remember much about the drive," I said. "The rain was so heavy. All I know is that we were definitely going the wrong way." I'd been scared, claustrophobic in that hammering downpour, and I'd had other things on my mind.

I could hear the rushing noise of the river before I saw it. We rounded a bend and there it was: a deep, fast-moving, brown-grey stream with occasional crests of white. It must have been thirty yards across. Looking at it made me feel strange, and very small, and as if I shouldn't have been alive now. How had either Bulewi or I survived being swept downstream in those torrential waters?

I was acutely aware of Nicholas's presence beside me and thought he might have been observing me as I stared at the water. I did not dare to look back. Instead, I decided to take a photo of the river to send to Vince as proof. I took out my phone and turned it on. Immediately it beeped, signaling I had a message, and my hands began to tremble. I didn't have just one message. I had six of them from Vince.

I didn't want to listen to them. Couldn't. Instead I navigated to the camera facility on the phone and took a few pictures. In the poor light and with such basic photographic equipment, they were not great, but at least the road leading to the river could be clearly seen, and the road leading away on its other side was distinguishable.

Then I hurriedly switched off the phone, worried that Vince would call me yet again because I felt incapable of speaking to him now. I needed some time alone first, to process what had happened. To work out exactly why I'd allowed that forbidden kiss.

I knew now that I must confront Nicholas on the drive back to the lodge and explain where I stood. Apologize, and tell him that despite all the evidence to the contrary, I really wasn't interested in taking him up on his audacious offer.

Lightning flickered in the clouds and I flinched as a huge clap of thunder split the air.

"You okay?" Nicholas asked, his voice like a caress, and I knew he wasn't only referring to the sudden noise.

"I'm fine," I replied. Aware that my voice had sounded sharp, I added, "Thank you."

"We'd better get back. Storm's coming," he said.

He turned the car around and headed away from the surging waters.

The wheels skidded on the steep uphill road, spinning in a section of deep, slippery mud. I caught my breath, picturing vividly what might happen if we were trapped here in the rain while the river rose again.

Completely focused on the treacherous path ahead, Nicholas engaged four wheel drive and carefully eased the big vehicle sideways, then forward again. The tires bit into the soft going, suddenly finding the grip they needed as he coaxed it patiently through the sticky patch.

"Nothing to worry about," he reassured me as we drove onto firmer ground. "This vehicle can handle far worse terrain."

I wanted to tell him that it was as much the driver's skill as the car's capability that had taken us so smoothly through the danger. But my words were silenced as Nicholas placed his hand on my leg.

It rested there, just above my knee, warm and firm, while the car jounced over a large bump in the road and my stomach jolted just as hard, though for different reasons. I could not suppress the flood of lust I felt at his caress. It was as if that light touch was sending a message— a subtle signal with sex as its underscore—to every cell in my body.

Staring down, I noticed again the beautiful squareness of his tanned hand, with long, strong fingers that looked as if they might equally belong to an artist or an engineer.

"You're an interesting woman, Erin," he observed. Now those fingers were lightly stroking over the thin beige fabric of the borrowed shorts I wore. The action was having the most unprecedented effect on my body. My skin was tingling at his touch, my jaw was dropping open, while my heart was hammering with excitement.

"Trust me, I don't often get no for an answer, but when I do, I respect it," he continued. "But you're sending me mixed messages. It would be wrong of me not to try to figure them out. To explore the limits of your permissiveness."

His voice caressed the last word. The stroking exploration of his fingers had reached the inside of my thigh. I was absolutely paralyzed. My carefully built defenses had crumbled at his touch. The overpowering sense of shame that filled me at what I was allowing him to do—the fact that I could not tell him to stop—did not in any way lessen the deep, hot lust that pooled in the pit of my belly.

"Eland on your left," he said gently, as his touch moved up and I felt his fingertips brush, briefly and deliciously, over the crotch of my shorts, the action sending a pulse of liquid pleasure through me. I caught my breath, my brain processing his words far too slowly, and turned my head to see that yes, there was some sort of large antelope standing a few feet from the road and observing the leisurely progress of the Land Cruiser.

I gripped the sides of the leather seat as his fingers returned to their exploration, stroking over the place where the soft fabric covered the rounded lips of my sex, each small movement of his hand creating a flood of sensation that washed through me. My heartbeat was rapid, my nipples felt tight and aching, but the rest of my body was melting, languorous, utterly incapable of resistance.

He stroked his hand gently upwards, massaging the softness of my pubic area, before moving it to the waistband of my shorts. Deftly, he undid the belt and eased the zipper down. Neither of us spoke. The only sound was the soft swishing and scrunching of the tires over the mud and the stones, and the rumble of thunder overhead. The air felt heavy and close, as if the clouds were pressing in to cover us, concealing our actions from the outside world.

With every heart-pounding second that passed, I had the opportunity to consider what my consent meant—both now, and in the long term—but the frantic guilt that was drumming in my brain was smothered and silenced by the boiling desire that the moment offered.

The waistband of my shorts gaped open now and his fingers slipped inside. His touch felt warm and sure. He caressed the skin of my lower belly and the pulse deep in my groin intensified to a painful throbbing.

"Almost completely shaved," he whispered, running his fingers over the narrow strip of hair above my cleft, and then over the hairless skin surrounding it. "You feel so silken smooth. So soft." His hand pressed gently on my pubic bone, his fingers massaging the tender flesh.

Crazy thoughts spun in my mind. I should pull myself out of the moment, make a witty comment about the thoughtfulness of him having provided a razor in my bathroom, I should tell him to stop. Each and every one of these thoughts was overridden, as his hand moved lower, by the compelling need of my body.

Instead, I let out a moan as his finger parted my lips and slid between them; a moan that was echoed by Nicholas as he felt the wetness there.

"God, Erin, you're so ready."

Ready to accept his most intimate sexual advances? Oh, this was bad. *I* was bad. As he stirred the tip of his finger lusciously inside the cleft of my moistened slit, I arched my hips toward him, turning to him, my eyes wide, my lips apart.

"Yes," Nicholas whispered. Rain splattered onto the windscreen, the storm closing in on us with violence, the flicking of the wipers unable to keep up with its assault. It drummed on the roof and poured over the leaves and grasses around us. The car had become a capsule in a deafening tunnel of grayness. How was he managing to keep it on the road as well as do this to me? Jesus, I had no idea, but right then, I'd have chosen pleasure over safety all the way.

He slid a finger inside me, teasing, pulling it out when he heard my small cry of delight before slipping it in again, this time deeper. I was pressed back in my seat, my back arched, my hips pushed toward him, proving to him I was open, available, wanting. Silently begging for him.

He slid two fingers inside me, pushing them deep, circling them in a slow, luscious motion so that they grazed over erogenous zones I hadn't known existed, causing muscles inside me to spasm with desire.

"Fuck," Nicholas whispered. He yanked the wheel to the left so that we juddered off the road and splashed through puddles. He stamped on the brake, causing water to shoot from under the heavy tires, before cutting the engine. "Jesus, Erin. You're so turned on, I can feel you clenching around me. Do you know how hot that is?"

He twisted around, moving to face me, thrusting one of his legs over the passenger seat and across mine so he was sprawled over me. In the confined space of the car I could feel the body heat radiating from him. I was drowning in his eyes. The rain was hissing around us, cutting off all visibility outside. This was a hurricane… a monsoon.

I gasped as Nicholas's fingers angled inside me to caress again and again over a pulsatingly sensitive nerve center. His thumb was circling my clitoris in a slow spiral of delight. I tensed my stomach muscles, desperately trying to hold myself back from the pleasure, trying to stop the inevitable, but he was onto me.

"I want to see you orgasm," he whispered. "And you're going to, Erin. You can try to resist it if you like. The longer you fight your body, the harder you'll come in the end. Or else…" his thumb stroked me in a silken rhythm, in time with the soft pumping of his fingers. The thundering of my own heartbeat had made me forget the storm outside. "Or else you could just let it happen."

My lips had fallen open. I gasped in shuddery breaths. Abruptly, the car's temperature seemed to ratchet up to double what it had been. I thrust myself onto his fingers, feeling the pleasure inside me escalate to boiling point and then, with a cry, I gave myself up to my climax, staring helplessly into his eyes, bucking my hips hard against his hand as the peaks of pleasure shocked through me.

He slowly withdrew his fingers, lifted them to his mouth and sucked them. Gently, his fingertips traced the outline of my face. Then he leaned forward and kissed me deeply and hard, with the same raw urgency I'd seen in his expression. I could taste myself on his lips. I wanted to keep kissing him… I wanted more from him, and could feel how badly he wanted me.

But, far too late, I found myself able to break the kiss and whisper, "Enough."

Thunder crashed around us.

Nicholas let out a deep breath. He nodded, then shifted back into the driver's seat, started the car, and eased it back onto the slippery road.

I zipped my shorts up again. We drove on in silence. As the pleasure of my orgasm ebbed, in its place came sharp, shameful regret. As the heavy vehicle splashed through the deep puddles outside the main gates of the lodge, I found my eyes blurring with tears. I sniffed, blinking them away, and Nicholas glanced at me.

"You okay?" he asked softly.

"I'm fine," I muttered, but my voice was wobbly and he must have known my words were a lie. What did he care, in any case, I told myself. He'd made it clear upfront that he was only after one thing. Now he had another cheap thrill to add to the notches on his belt—and I had a burden of guilt which I could not deny or ignore.

Chief in my mind: what the hell should I tell Vince?

I didn't know. I needed to think about this, and urgently. Needed to sort out my head. My husband would be trying to call me again, growing more anxious and angrier with every minute that passed as he found my phone was still turned off.

When we parked in the garage, Nicholas turned to me and said, in a worried voice, "Erin, I…"

I didn't wait to hear what he had to say. I climbed out of the car, slammed the door, and, ducking my head against the blowing rain, jogged along the walkway before entering the house. I ran along the wide, tiled corridor to my bedroom and slammed the door behind me.

I'd thought I'd end up crying but now, surprisingly, the tears would not come. I lay there for a while, trapped in my tangled thoughts, before sitting bolt upright.

The helicopter.

Damn it all.

I needed to call Vince back and I had forgotten to ask about the fucking helicopter.

CHAPTER 8

I CALLED VINCE ANYWAY. It was the lesser of the two evils; the other being to go and look for Nicholas to ask him about the helicopter, and right then I could not face him.

I turned on the phone and quickly, before he could phone me again, dialed my husband.

The number rang and rang, my nerves cranking up tighter with each second that passed, until the call went through to voicemail.

Vince *always* answered his phone. What was wrong?

"Hi, babes," I said. "I saw you've been calling. Sorry I didn't have my phone on. I got a ride down to the river to get some photos of where the bridge was. I'll send them to you now. I hope you're doing fine. I love you. I miss you."

I disconnected. Now the tears were prickling. I forwarded the photos to his phone and watched while the messages went through. Then I listened to the messages he'd left, which were all a terse variation on the words, "Call me as soon as you can."

I didn't know what to make of what I had done with Nicholas, other than that it had been unforgivable. Panic churned inside me, intensified by the fact that, despite leaving multiple messages for me, Vince hadn't answered my call when I had phoned back. For now, I could not even try to make things right between us, but would have to stew in my emotions until he decided to contact me.

I wanted some support on this. God, I needed somebody to talk to, to help me sort my head out and give me some perspective. But who was there? Who could I tell?

My best friend, Samantha, would be the only person I'd confide in about something like this, but Samantha and I hadn't really spoken for a while. In fact, apart from when she'd attended our engagement party, we'd pretty much fallen out of contact in recent times. She was married, living in New Jersey, and had a baby girl. I thought perhaps little Jessica was keeping her too busy for her to stay in touch with friends. Or maybe it was my fault—that I'd been too focused on my husband and had neglected my other relationships. Either way, now was a good time to send her an email. I trusted Samantha's opinion. She would be able to offer me some good advice.

It took me a long time to compose the message and a lot of false starts, but eventually it was ready to go.

Hey Sam… how are you doing? Just wanted to catch up with you because we haven't spoken for ages. I'm stuck on a game farm in South Africa, if you can believe that! I mean really stuck—as in, on the wrong side of a washed away bridge. Things aren't going great at this moment between me and Vince, and this separation is not helping. And now I've got other complications, because the owner of the game farm is trying to get me into bed.

I stopped typing for a minute, overwhelmed by the shameful memory of how Nicholas had watched me orgasm, his eyes devouring me as I gave myself over to abandon. How he'd kissed me as the aftershocks of that incredible climax were still rippling through me. Better not to say any of that to Samantha, I decided.

Does this all sound like a soap opera? That's pretty much how I'm feeling now. There's so much I want to talk with you about—or write you about. Hope to hear from you soon!

I sent the mail. Then I tested the water in the shower. It was there, and it was hot. Quickly, I stepped under it.

I was out and dressed in fresh clothes when there was a tap on my bedroom door.

"Who is it?"

I felt my cheeks grow hot when I heard Nicholas's voice.

"I'm going to fix an early dinner in the kitchen. Come and eat."

"I'm not hungry, thanks," I called.

"Fine. I'll bring you something, then."

I let out an impatient sigh. It seemed that food was on the agenda, whether I wanted it or not.

"I'll be there in five," I told him.

✢ ✢ ✢

Nicholas was on his own in the kitchen, mixing ingredients in a bowl near the west window, through which I could see the setting sun blazing from under a mass of roiling clouds.

"Most of the staff here have Saturdays and Sundays off," he said. "So I do the cooking. Not gourmet style, I'm afraid. This evening, French toast is on the menu."

I hadn't even realized it was Saturday today.

I watched while Nicholas took the first of a pile of sourdough slices and dunked it in a mixture of egg and milk. On the gas stove, a heavy-bottomed frying pan was heating up.

"Please could you tell me if there's a helicopter available anywhere?" I said. "I really need to get across this river. I need to get back to my life."

"My helicopter is not available, I'm afraid," Nicholas said. "I've loaned it to the local police. One of my staff flew out with it early yesterday morning, before you had woken up."

"Oh," I said, deflated. "Do you know when it will be…?"

"No. It may be a few more days before I get it back." Turning his attention away from his cooking, he explained grimly, "Downriver from here, a community of two hundred people was washed away when the flooding started. Twenty of them are still missing. The others are stranded, and desperate for supplies. All they have are the clothes they were wearing. Whenever the weather allows, the police are flying food, fuel, and water to them, as well as running search and rescue and Medevac operations."

"Oh," I said, feeling ashamed to have asked a selfish question and for a moment, illogically angry at Vince for having pressured me into asking. I should have known—in some way, I had known—that if there had been transport available, I would already have been offered out of here.

"Guess we're stuck with each other for a while longer, then," I said, offering a wry smile.

"I guess we are."

Nicholas was wearing a faded green T-shirt that emphasized the deep tan of his arms. Vince, who was very wardrobe-conscious, wouldn't have been seen dead in a garment that showed so much wear, but Nicholas made the shirt look sexy. And I knew what was underneath it. I had seen his hard-muscled torso, had felt the breadth of his shoulders as I dug my fingers into them...

Oh, God, I urgently needed to do something to distract myself from him.

"Are we having any salad with that toast?" I asked.

"I wasn't planning to make any—I usually fry a couple of tomatoes—but salad's a good idea. Want some?"

"I'll make us some." Relieved to be able to focus on something other than the mouthwatering sight of Nicholas de Lanoy at work in his kitchen, I turned away and opened the fridge door.

After a quick hunt through, I removed a small head of lettuce, two tomatoes, a green pepper, a large, perfectly ripe avocado, and a tub of feta cheese, which from its handwritten label looked to have come from a local dairy. Nicholas passed me a chopping board and a knife. Our fingers brushed as I took the board. The touch was electric, and in my efforts to move my hand away fast, I dropped the knife, which clattered to the floor.

Unfazed by my clumsy attempt at avoiding contact with him, he picked the knife up, handed me another, and then showed me the cupboard which housed a selection of pottery and glass bowls. I chose an attractive glazed pottery bowl with a swirled pattern of earthen brown and cream.

"Can I please talk to you frankly?" I said as I began washing the lettuce.

"Go ahead." He placed the first two dripping slices of bread into the sizzling pan.

"Nicholas, I'm really sorry about what happened between us earlier today."

"Are you?" There was a flash of wicked humor in his smile as he turned to me. "I'm not." Focusing once again on his cooking, he slid another two slices of bread into the pan before adjusting the heat.

"Well, I am. I am regretting it deeply." I took a fast breath. "I am married."

"Like I told you, that's not an issue for me."

"It is for me. Look, I take my vows seriously."

"Why do you and your husband travel in separate cars, then?" Nicholas's voice was innocent.

My knife sank into a round of creamy feta, which I transferred from the tub to the board.

"We'd had a falling out. A fight."

"And does he always throw you out of the vehicle when that happens? Seems rather extreme to me."

"He didn't throw me out! He just…" I let out an impatient breath. "Look, any couple can fight, right?"

"You say so, Erin. Maybe you believe that. I personally don't agree. I don't think it is necessary. There are far more constructive and pleasant ways to spend time together than by fighting."

"Well, what would you know?" I hacked at the soft cheese with what felt like way too much force. "You told me yourself that you've mainly had short, no-strings affairs. A week of fun and then you or your partner moves on. If that's the case, then you've never had to see a relationship through difficult times."

Silence descended on the kitchen for a while, broken only by the blistering of the toast in the pan.

"Good point," Nicholas said eventually. "So you were going through a bad patch with your husband, but you love him, and you feel guilty about what you've done?"

"Yes." I cupped the avocado in my hand and sliced gently through its skin. "That's exactly how I feel. If I stay here—which I obviously don't have a choice about—there can be no more of this. I will not be the one to wreck my marriage."

"The way you say that implies it's heading for wreckage in any case. Are you going to wait and hope he does it first?"

"No," I snapped, annoyed. "That's not what I meant. Nobody is going to wreck this marriage. Not me, not you, and not my husband. I'm telling you how things are. And I'd appreciate your cooperation."

"Well, I can give you my personal guarantee that you're not going to get it," Nicholas said, and I stared at him, wide-eyed with shock at his words. He didn't meet my gaze. He was busy flipping the toast.

"How—what do you mean?"

Abandoning his cooking, he swung round to face me.

"You are an incredibly sexy woman," he said in a low voice. "There's… I think there's a powerful connection between us, Erin. I don't know what the hell it is or why it's there. You have been driving me just about crazy with desire to get you into bed. Right now, I'm pretty much incapable of thinking straight, and I'm certainly unwilling to make any effort to go along with what you're asking."

I was briefly silenced by the effect of his words, and the realization that I'd been driving him as crazy with lust as he was driving me. Seriously? I'd done that to him? His confession was a powerful turn-on, so much so that I forgot to be angry about his brazen defiance of my wishes.

Turning back to the stove, Nicholas slid the spatula under the bread and transferred the crisp, browned slices to a plate.

"If you want to stay away from me, that's your choice," he continued. "But you're the one who's been sending me mixed messages. I don't know if you're going to change that from now on—but if the message is yes, I'm not going to say no. No way."

He flipped the final slice of toast onto the plate and then, to my surprise, sprinkled them with sea salt and a grind of black pepper. He picked up the plate, placed it on a tray with two others, knives, and forks, and walked to the arched doorway leading to the lounge.

"When that salad's ready, do you want to bring it outside? And there's a jug in the fridge with some freshly made lemonade."

For a moment, I stood, torn between following him through the lounge to the outside veranda or marching back to my room in a huff. Eventually, hunger and common-sense won the battle. He was right. The decisions I would make now were up to me. There was no reason to ask for his help in this. It was sufficient for me to know that, for as long as I was able to resist him, he would not make the first advance.

Or so I hoped.

Five minutes later, our simple but delectable-looking meal was arranged on the oval wooden table under the covered balcony from where I could see the last deep scarlet rays of the setting sun. I added olive oil and balsamic to the salad before tossing it, and Nicholas forked two generously sized pieces of toast onto each plate.

"This is delicious," I said, cutting off another large chunk and transferring it to my mouth as soon as I'd swallowed the first.

I was a naturally fast eater. In fact, Vince was constantly telling me to behave more like a lady when I ate so as not to humiliate him in front of other people, and to take more time over my meals. And so, to please him, for the past few months I had picked delicately at food I would previously have devoured with gusto. Now, I realized that there was no need to do this here—in fact, the opposite was indicated, since I wanted to steer away from anything that might make me look more feminine or appealing in Nicholas's eyes.

"The salad's great, Erin. Very tasty. I didn't know you were a cook."

Perhaps he was just trying to flatter me, but even so I felt a glow of pride at his words. It felt good to have my cooking complimented, even if it had only consisted of chopping things up. I'd given up trying to cook for Vince—I could never prepare food the way he liked it, so we usually ordered takeout from one of the nearby restaurants.

"Thank you," I said. "It's easy with such wonderful ingredients. How many of them come from the garden?"

"Most of them. The cheese is from down the road and the olive oil and balsamic are brought in from an organic estate in the Cape that I have an investment in. The bowl itself is made by the women from a small community near here."

"The bowl is really pretty. And I see it's part of a set with the plates. Do they sell a lot of them?"

"Yes. They're doing extremely well. They do bowls and dishes of all sizes, cups, and mugs. The crockery is sold in a lot of the gift shops and used by a number of the guest houses in the area, and they're getting more and more orders for complete sets, to be shipped to various countries overseas."

"You sound very proud of them. Are you involved in that project?"

He nodded. "I am. I helped them start the venture just two years ago. It was one of my first investments, actually."

"That's really good to hear." So Nicholas was a businessman—although, from what he'd said, this was a relatively new career. How did this fit in with being a trained paramedic who'd worked abroad? And, clearly, he was extremely wealthy—where had his money come from?

I was curious to know more, but at the same time found myself reluctant to ask. After all, there was no point in finding out anything about Nicholas when I was actively trying to remain uninvolved.

I speared the last piece of cheese on my plate before putting my knife and fork down. I had my eye on one of the two remaining pieces of toast, but first I was going to have the last few swallows of the tart, tasty lemonade.

"Have more," Nicholas encouraged me. "I've been enjoying watching you eat. I like it that you love your food. I always think…" He stopped himself.

"You think what?" I transferred a third piece of toast to my plate.

"No. I shouldn't tell you."

I glowered at him. "Now you have to."

"I always think the way a woman eats her food is an indication of how she makes love," he said in a low voice, his eyes gleaming.

"You were right. You shouldn't have told me." It was strange how, just by saying those words, he'd been able to fill me with a sense of shivering expectancy. Suddenly, I felt as if I was in an elevator that was ascending too fast.

"You are sensual. Open. Greedy." His smile flashed again. "And that's a compliment, to be taken in the best possible way."

Oh, crap. My decision not to eat in a ladylike manner had back-fired on me horribly, and now my face felt so hot, it must look crim-son—and it wasn't the only part of me that was experiencing a sud-den increase in blood flow. I shifted in my seat, hoping to banish the overpowering sense of lust that his words had induced. Really, what *was* it about this man?

You're the only one who can make the decision to stop, I told myself.

"Greedy, maybe," I replied, changing the subject. "But I love ex-ercise as much as I love food. Is it safe to go walking around here? I'd say running, but you don't seem to have any sports shoes available in my size."

Nicholas gave a rueful nod. "That's a pity. Anyway, there's a four-mile paved track that runs between the garden and the surrounding bushveld. If you stick to that, you should be fine during daylight hours. In fact, the paving's so smooth you could probably run it bare-foot. Beyond that, there are unpaved paths that lead deeper into the bush, but it would be better not to walk too far alone, even though there are no predators in this fenced area. The black rhino are more timid than the white ones, but any one of the Big Five can be danger-ous if it's suddenly surprised."

"Thank you," I said. "I'll walk the track tomorrow."

"If you prefer exercising indoors, there is a gym here as well," he told me. "It's in the east wing of the lodge. It's not fully equipped, but there are some weights, and some cardiovascular equipment. A couple of spinning bicycles, rowing machines, and so on."

"Great. I'll give that a try, too."

We were both finished eating. I stacked the dishes and took them back to the kitchen.

"You can leave them in the sink," he said. "They'll be washed in the morning."

"Well, good night," I told him, feeling suddenly uneasy. "Thanks for the dinner, and for—er—for being so honest with me."

"Pleasure," he said. There was maybe a foot of distance separating us and I could have sworn I could see the air shimmering with the force of our awareness for each other. Being near him was dangerous. It was compelling me to step toward him; to melt into his arms.

"Good night," I said. Summoning every scrap of my willpower, I walked away, through the kitchen, hearing his "Good night," behind me but not turning round.

I made it back to my room feeling flushed and unsettled, seriously frustrated, but yet oddly triumphant, as if, despite all the odds, I'd won a war with my body. It was early still—only seven p.m. I tried Vince's number again but, as I'd expected and feared, it rang unanswered.

I left another brief message, then checked my email.

Samantha had replied.

Hey girlfriend! Great to hear from you! But so sorry you're in a such a difficult situation there. What's up? You sound like you're traveling solo, not with Vince? What's gone wrong between you two? And who's this man that's trying to get you into bed? Please tell me more. I'd love to try and help—or offer you a shoulder to cry on. Chat later… got to run now; lunch is being demanded at high volume!! Xxx.

I couldn't help feeling a sense of crushing relief as I read this. I had forgotten how wonderful Sam was… how loyal and supportive. How long since I'd spoken to her? Far too long. In fact, thinking back on it, when I'd moved in with Vince soon after we'd met, I'd fallen out of touch with all my friends. As soon as I got back home, a visit to Sam was in order.

I'd email her again in the morning, I decided. Hopefully by then Vince would have called me back and we would have talked things through and I'd be able to offer Sam the reassuring news that everything was fine.

I'd been able to spend an evening with Nicholas without succumbing to his charms. And, next time, it would be easier. I'd done it once… how difficult could it be to do it again?

Ten minutes later I was in bed.

And that was when the thoughts of him filled my sleepless mind, unstoppable and undeniable, causing me to realize that the pleasure he'd given me this morning had only been enough to whet my appetite.

This man, this amoral Nicholas de Lanoy, was revealing to me a more rapaciously sexual side than I'd ever known I possessed. I caught my breath as the memories of what we'd done replayed themselves in my mind. The way his fingers had felt thrusting deep inside me… the urgency of the desire I'd seen in his eyes.

There was no way I was going to sleep—not now, not staring up at the darkened ceiling and thinking about how he had sucked the taste of me from his hand before kissing me deeply… I drew a shuddering breath. I honestly couldn't remember the last time in my life when I'd felt so aroused… and when the object of my sexual frustration was under the same roof as me. Perhaps when I'd been sixteen and at summer camp.

Well, at least I could do something about it now. And I intended to. To stop myself from going insane with frustration, I was going to masturbate to the fantasy of making love to Nicholas… and at this hour of the night, I could be certain nobody was going to be knocking on my door and interrupting me. Although… imagine if Nicholas himself did just that.

Lust flooded me as I thought of him slipping between the sheets beside me, in total darkness. No words would need to be said; we'd both know why he was here. With the intense urgency sparked by prolonged denial, he'd be kissing me deeply, possessing my mouth with his own. And I would run my hands over his incredible body, learning the feel of him, the smell of him, knowing that as I pressed my fingers into the taut muscles of his back and caressed his firm buttocks, my touch would be fuelling his desire.

I caught my breath as I visualized his hands instead of my own now stroking between my moistened, swollen lips. And if, this time, his expert fingering was only serving to prepare me for the bigger, deeper penetration to follow…

My breathing grew faster as I remembered how he'd felt when he pressed himself against me while we were in the swimming pool—thick, hard, aroused.

Oh God, what would he feel like inside me? The thought of making love with… no, of fucking this lustful stranger was causing a sheen of sweat to appear on my skin. It would never happen in real life. I was going to make sure of that. But it was happening now, in my mind, and I intended to let it go all the way. I was going to immerse myself in the fantasy of raw sex with Nicholas de Lanoy in the hope that I'd finally be able to rid myself of this seemingly unquenchable desire.

Thrusting two fingers inside myself, grinding my pelvis into my cupped hand to satisfy the throbbing need of my clitoris, I came hard, breathlessly, my body convulsing as I sobbed with pleasure at the release. My heart was pounding fast, and I kicked the sheets aside to cool myself. Then I lay, feeling the aftershocks spasm through me. Despite all my efforts to ban him from my thoughts, I found myself wishing that Nicholas was there to taste my arousal as he'd done so sensually before.

Sleep followed sometime after, and I didn't know how much later it was when the shrill ringing of my phone wrenched me out of my dreams.

CHAPTER 9

I GROPED GROGGILY IN the direction of the noise and succeeded in knocking the phone off the bedside table. It hit the floor with a clatter but the ringing didn't stop. I fumbled for the light switch, turned it on, and squinting in the bright glow, peered over the edge of the bed until I located the instrument, which seemed to have been ringing forever. Hastily, I answered.

"Hello?"

"So don't you call me by my name any more?"

It was Vince. Hearing him, relief filled me... he'd at least called back, even though he was still moody.

"I was fast asleep when I heard the phone," I explained.

"Is that so? Who else did you think would be calling?"

"Well, the insurance company, maybe." Damn. Wider awake now, I could have kicked myself for not realizing it would have been Vince. Now, his suspicions were inflamed again. He clearly thought that I had been expecting somebody else to call.

To my relief, he didn't dwell on my slip-up.

"I was out late doing the shoot. We put up lights and worked through the evening and into the night."

"Oh, wonderful, Vince. That's so exciting. How did it go? Did you get some good images?"

"I got some great shots. But I need another assistant."

"Huh?" I frowned, taking a moment to process the words, before realizing with a stab of surprise, that he was implying *I* would have been his…

No. Surely not.

"What do you mean, 'assistant'?"

"Well, you tell me you're stranded elsewhere," he responded coldly.

"But I wasn't going to be your assistant!" My voice sounded very loud in the quiet house. "I was going to be your partner. We were doing this fashion shoot as a team. I mean—sure, I was going to help you, but you said this was going to be a showcase of both our talent…"

With an effort, I cut myself short. Now was not the time to pick a fight, even though his words had hurt me. Probably he hadn't meant them that way. And I knew Vince preferred to work with somebody helping him. Realistically, as I had done before so many times, I would have ended up filling that role.

"I'm sorry," I told him. "I'm glad you have at least done some productive work."

"I'm thinking of flying Helena out here. She got in touch yesterday and said she was in the country at the moment. In Cape Town."

"Helena?"

"You know," he said. "That model I was dating a while back. Oh, hang on a sec. The studio in New York is calling in."

Abruptly, I was switched over to the "on hold" signal and waited, seething, for him to return to the phone. I knew about Helena—I'd seen many photos of her in Vince's portfolio and he'd spoken of her often, telling me about the stormy relationship they'd had, and how he'd broken her heart by leaving her because she was never going to understand him well enough. She was my physical opposite, with warm brown eyes, deeply tanned skin, platinum hair, and breasts that had been artificially enhanced to D-cups.

This was really unfair. I wanted to lash out at him for his double standards. We had rules in place regarding exes—rules that Vince himself had laid out.

I had been told that contact with previous partners was forbidden, because he believed that it could and would lead to infidelity. I had agreed to this unwillingly, because I'd stayed good and platonic friends with a couple of my exes, but it was surely not worth jeopardizing my marriage over it.

The point had been driven home to me just a month ago when I'd taken a call from an unfamiliar number one evening, only to hear the cheery voice of Mike, an ex-boyfriend I'd dated briefly when I was twenty-one and who was now married to another good friend of mine. Mike had been phoning to let me know he'd changed jobs, and that he and Jen would be in New York after Christmas and wanted to get together with me.

"Mike!" I'd exclaimed, thrilled to hear his voice. I was delighted he'd gotten in touch, and couldn't help feeling relieved that he'd called just after Vince had left the apartment to go to a meeting. We'd spoken for a few minutes—he'd updated me on how Jen was doing, and I told him that I was now married.

"Married?" Mike echoed. "Hey, did you elope, or what? How about our promise to go to each other's weddings?"

Mike had invited me to his, but I hadn't done the same. My wedding had been attended by my mother, my aunt, and many of Vince's friends and family. Inviting one of my exes wouldn't have been acceptable to Vince, and the last thing I'd wanted was to cause friction on that special day.

"Yeah, I guess you could say we eloped," I said in a small voice.

Then, to my horror, I'd glanced round to see Vince standing in the bedroom doorway, watching me. His face was dark with fury and the expression in his eyes had caused my stomach to tighten almost painfully.

"Anyway," I continued quickly, desperate to implement some hasty damage control. "I've got to go. I'm glad you and your wife are doing well. But I don't think it's appropriate to meet up with exes. Please don't call me again."

Mike had said goodbye, sounding hurt and confused, just before I slammed the phone down. Immediately, Vince's inquisition had started. "Why was he calling you at all? Why did he want to give you his new number? Why did he think you'd be available to see him?"

Defending myself had been exhausting, and my efforts to make him understand had been futile. He had simply refused to believe I'd been telling the truth. His anger had become so immense, so vicious, that I had burst into tears under its onslaught. Even that had not been enough to deflect his intent, and I remember fearing at one stage that he might hit me.

He hadn't, although at one point he had grabbed me by my shoulders hard enough to leave bruises, before shaking me like a rag doll until my head spun.

The next day, when we had made up, he had been back to the normal, focused, serious, and driven Vince that I adored. Before he'd started working on a stunning series of new images, he'd apologized for losing his temper and I, in turn, had said I was sorry for having caused the problem in the first place.

"I don't know why you put up with me when I can be so difficult," he'd remarked darkly, swiveling his chair round to face his computer screen. "I'm too much for you to handle, Erin. You should look for somebody else. I don't know if we rushed into this commitment too quickly."

"No!" I'd exclaimed in a panic—what *was* he suggesting? That we split up when we'd only just gotten *married*? That I wasn't able to deal with him? Of course I was—more than able, and I intended to try even harder to prove it.

Speaking fast, I continued, "We're perfect for each other, Vince! And I can handle you—of course I can. I love you. I love being with you. You are my soul mate. The person I waited twenty-seven years of my life to meet. I will never, ever leave you."

Vince had turned away from his work. He stood up, wrapped his arms around me, and pressed his head into my shoulder. We stayed like that for a long while, with me blinking tears of relief out of my eyes at his uncharacteristic display of vulnerability. I had never loved him more fiercely than I did at that moment, and I had resolved that I was never going to let a similar situation happen again.

Later in the day, I'd emailed those exes I was still in contact with, including Mike, and asked them please not to call me in future, but instead to communicate via email, and only then if there was a pressing reason they needed to get in touch.

I hadn't heard back from any of them, and knew I'd had no right to feel hurt over Mike's silence. Not that I'd had much time to feel hurt. It was as if being married to Vince had become my full time job—but it was a job I loved and I intended to do it to the best of my ability. Enjoying all our good moments. Managing his moods. Going with him everywhere…

"Hi." Vince's voice on the line interrupted my thoughts, dragging me back to my present circumstances. Finally, he'd finished speaking with the studio.

I gathered my courage together. I so seldom spoke up against Vince that I didn't know how I should start. But surely a marriage was also about balance and compromise, and in this case I felt he was upsetting the balance and needed to compromise.

"Don't you think what you're doing is unfair?" I asked.

"What do you mean?" He sounded defensive. I guessed he knew exactly what I meant.

"Why are there two sets of rules here, Vince? I'm not allowed to speak to exes, but you are. I'm not allowed to have contact with male friends, but you can get in touch with your female ones. Even though, as you yourself said, it can lead to infidelity."

My words were strong, but all the same I felt uneasy saying them, knowing how hypocritical they were given the events that had played out earlier today.

"I know I can trust myself," Vince responded, his voice icy. "Have I ever flirted with another woman when you've been around?"

"I…" Well, no, he hadn't. But he'd certainly spoken to other women socially, and given his star status, they tended to fawn over him—often even while I was with him. I guessed that when that happened, it didn't count as flirting, though.

"All right." With a sense of relief, I found myself backing down. "I was just checking. As long as you get the shoot done."

"I might not need to fly her up here if you can get back in time. Did you ask about the helicopter?"

"I did. Nicholas says it's not available. It's being used to fly emergency supplies to another stranded community."

As I finished speaking the words, I realized my slip-up. I clapped a hand over my mouth, feeling a cold rush of terror flood through me.

"Nicholas? Who's Nicholas?" Vince's words were like blades.

For a moment I couldn't speak. I was too panicked by my mistake. Then, desperately trying to keep my voice calm, I responded. "I'm sure I told you. He's Mrs. de Lanoy's husband."

"Strange that you're on first name terms with him but not with her," he observed, icily.

"The staff all refer to him as Mr. Nicholas. For all I know, his surname could be something different from his wife's," I replied, noticing my hands had started trembling. "If and when I see him again, I'll make sure to ask."

"You do that," he said. "You go ahead, Erin. Tell me whatever lies you like. Do you really think I believe you? I'm going to find out where you really are, and you and I are going to have a lot to talk about when you're out of there."

"Vince, I…"

"I have to go," he snapped. "I've got New York on the line again."

And, just like that, he disconnected.

CHAPTER 10

FOR WHAT FELT LIKE an hour but was probably more like thirty seconds, I paced the room, my stomach churning as I came to the realization that there was only one thing I could do.

I desperately needed Vince to believe my story. But if he searched online, he would discover the truth.

Five pages into Google—yup. He'd sounded like a man who would search five pages in, just to prove his point.

I pulled on some shorts and the sandals. Then, flashlight in hand, I left the room.

The passage was in complete darkness, lit only by the wavering beam of the flashlight and the faint shimmer of moonlight that brightened the windows. And I had no idea where Nicholas's bedroom might be.

I peered into the darkness, pushing my hair away from my face. Straight ahead was the dining room. Then the wide corridor branched to the left and the right. Which direction? Guessing right first, I made my way as quietly as possible along the tiled walkway.

Ahead of me, on the left and the right of the passage, were two white-painted wooden doors, both closed. Could one of these be his? Or would it be more likely that a master bedroom would be located at the end of the corridor?

I tapped quietly on one of the doors, just to check.

"Nicholas?" I said softly.

No reply. I could hear nothing except the faint trilling of the cicadas from outside the large window further down the passage.

I continued on my way, past the spill of light from the window, and back into shadowed darkness. Ahead of me was another door, right at the end of the corridor. My flashlight beam lit up the darkness of an open doorway and then trembled over the muscular form and tanned limbs of the man standing outside it, clad only in a pair of black silk boxers.

"Erin," Nicholas said, his voice low but hard. "I heard a noise. I was just coming out to see what it was. Is everything all right?"

"Everything's fine," I said. "I—I need to ask you a favor, though."

"A favor? Come on in." He stepped aside. I was intensely aware of his nearness as I walked past him and into the darkened room. I was careful not to brush against him, nor to give any signal that might cause him to misconstrue the reason for my visit. Thank God he didn't know that just a few hours ago I'd made myself come thinking of him and me together. Now I felt shamed by what I'd done—by how vividly and explicitly I'd imagined him as a lover.

I heard the flick of a lighter, and lowered my flashlight as a gas lamp on the table near the fireplace began to burn. Its flame illuminated the king-sized four-poster with its bedcovers rumpled, the luxurious-looking black leather sofa, the modern, glass-topped desk and director's chair, and the tall standard lamp in the corner. On the floor in front of the sofa was a large Persian rug.

He gestured toward the sofa, and as I sat down, I noticed the blank expanse of a massive wall-mounted screen on the opposite side.

"That is one enormous television," I said. "In the bedroom?"

Now, the hardness was gone from Nicholas's voice and it was filled with amusement. "War criminals have been sentenced for more minor offenses," he responded, seating himself at the other end of the couch.

"Sorry." I found myself smiling. Amazingly, my nervousness had eased, even if only temporarily. "I didn't mean…"

"If it makes you feel any better, I hardly ever watch the damned thing. It came with the house, like everything else. I've been meaning to get it moved into the lounge and replace it with a bookcase." He shifted to face me and I heard him take a breath. "So. To what do I owe the pleasure of your unexpected company?"

"I need to ask you a favor."

"Fire ahead."

"A very urgent one." Now I drew an audible breath. "And a very unusual one."

"What is it?"

"Nicholas…" I shook my head as if reaching a reluctant conclusion with myself. Asking the favor without explaining the situation wasn't going to work. I'd have to give him a bit of background.

"My husband and I, as you know, were having a fight at the time when we crossed the bridge," I said.

"Go on."

"He's a—possessive person. That's what our fight was about. And I'd prefer it if he didn't know that I've been spending this time with a handsome, available man."

Nicholas's teeth glinted. "You can count on my discretion in that regard. As I said, once you're gone, I won't ever contact you again if you don't want me to."

"What I need goes beyond that." I sighed again. God, this was hard work, and surprisingly embarrassing, too.

"How do you mean?"

"I've told him you're married. I've told him I've been dealing mostly with your wife."

"My wife?" Surprise filled Nicholas's voice, and in spite of the aching awkwardness of the situation, I found myself laughing. He sounded serious when he spoke again, though.

"What are you afraid of, Erin?"

"Nothing, really," I said quickly. "I made up Mrs. de Lanoy. To—to make sure that he wouldn't worry about me being here, on my own, away from him."

"You're weaving a tangled web."

"I am, and it gets worse."

"Go on." His eyes flicked briefly toward the darkened screen. "This is far more interesting than television could ever be."

"I Googled you," I whispered, and I was glad of the muted light because I could feel my face flaming.

"You did? And what did you find?" I didn't miss the sudden sharpness in his voice.

"Well, I Googled the lodge, actually, but your name came up. On the fifth page, there was a piece by an Australian journalist, written about six months ago. It was the only thing I could find online that hinted at the fact you might not be happily married."

Nicholas laughed. "The one by Angela? Yes, she sent me the piece to read before she posted it online. It did mention that fact, I remember."

"Could you possibly contact her—look, I know you don't stay in touch with your lovers, I know you've told me all of that—but as a huge favor to me, could you ask her to pull that piece? Just for a few weeks, until we're well away from here."

His brow creased. "You don't think you're being paranoid?"

"I don't." I was twisting my fingers together, a nervous habit I thought I'd left behind in my teens but which I'd found myself doing more and more frequently over the past few months. "He—my husband Vince has done this before. Googling, I mean."

Nicholas was quiet for a while. "And have you done this before?"

"Done what? Asked someone to remove content...?"

"No, I don't mean that. I mean given him a reason to Google."

"Never. Well, not until today, when you..." Now I was surprised my face wasn't lighting up the whole room with its embarrassed glow. "There have been times he's accused me of flirting but it's just his insecurity."

Nicholas was quiet for a few moments.

"This is really important to you, isn't it?"

"It is."

He looked at me for a few moments longer. Then he gave a small nod.

"Give me a sec."

He got up, walked over to the phone on his bedside table, and spent a minute searching through the contact list before dialing. I'd assumed he would go outside to take the call, or somewhere private at least, but he didn't. He stood by the window while he spoke. It would be late morning in Australia, I calculated, so at least he wouldn't be waking her up.

"Hey Ang, Nicholas here," he said, when the call was answered. "Yes, it really is me. No, I'm not in Sydney. How are things going with you?" He waited, listened. "Glad to hear it. Yes, fine on my side. I have a question to ask you, though. The piece you wrote on your blog—would you mind pulling it for a while?"

He paused, smiled. "It's as a favor to somebody else. No, not that kind of somebody." He laughed. "Perhaps," he said. "A boy can dream. Thanks. Could you possibly do it now? You're a star. Have a good day."

He disconnected and replaced the phone on the table.

"Done. Or it should be in the next few minutes."

His words lifted a huge weight of worry from my shoulders. "Thank you. I really appreciate it."

"It'll still be cached. Somebody who knows how to look for it could find it. Nothing ever disappears from the Internet entirely."

"I don't think Vince is that computer savvy. I'm sure this will be fine. Really, thank you."

I got up, but before I could leave Nicholas crossed the room and stood by the door. He looked down at me. In the flickering lamplight I saw his blond hair was tousled and every line of his sculpted body looked perfect. It scared me, how badly I wanted to touch him—and now that he'd already pleasured me so intimately, my inhibitions seemed to have weakened. It seemed natural for me to want to step forward into his embrace.

I knotted my fingers tightly into the edges of the T-shirt to give them something else to do.

"Erin, listen to me. You're in a bad situation here," he said in a low voice.

"I…" My voice was suddenly hoarse.

"You're married to a jealous man," he told me.

I looked down. "I know. I can handle it. A little jealousy is…"

"A little jealousy is not Googling the place where your wife has been stranded because you suspect her of infidelity. A little jealousy wouldn't bring you to my bedroom at midnight, begging for my help in deleting an old Internet article."

"I can handle it," I said again.

"You're already guilty," he said, and I blinked up at him as the reality of his words hit home. "If it's gone this far, your husband has already judged you. In his mind, you have been unfaithful. Nothing you can say or do is going to convince him otherwise. And it's a pity… because you're a beautiful woman."

I didn't know what to say. His words had silenced me. After a short pause, he continued.

"Clearly, despite his unreasonable behavior, you are being faithful to him. He should be proud of you. Hell, if nothing else, he should be frantically worried about you, stranded here after almost drowning."

"I didn't tell him I almost drowned."

"Why?" His eyes were pale and piercing. "To save him the distress? Is that why? Or was it because you wanted to spare him the truth that you had another man's lips on yours? Another man's hands on your body?"

He stared at me, and I knew he could see the answer in my face.

"Christ," he said forcefully. "You kept the fact you were resuscitated from him because you didn't want him to imagine somebody else touching you?"

"I… he probably wouldn't have minded, but…"

"Erin, that is not a normal reaction."

"You don't understand." Now I could feel tears prickling my eyes.

"Clearly, no."

"Most of the time our marriage is perfect. We're soul mates. It's just occasionally he gets insecure. This was one of those times. He's a wonderful, special, loving man."

"I'm sure he's a prince," Nicholas said dryly.

"Well, I can tell you one thing for sure. He's a better, more faithful husband than you would ever be," I spat.

His eyes narrowed and I knew my comment had struck home. Before he could answer, I turned and marched out of the bedroom.

CHAPTER 11

I WOKE EARLY THE next morning, still angry about what Nicholas had said the previous night. I decided to go for a quick walk and then spend the day right here, in my room. I did not want to speak to Nicholas. Not today, not for the rest of my stay here.

Not for the rest of my life.

Even the thought of what he'd said made me bristle with anger. What right did he have to criticize my husband? No doubt, this was all part of his seduction technique. Plan B, to be used if the straightforward approach failed. Drive a wedge between the lady and her man by making out that he's a jealous bastard who's going to think the worst of her no matter what.

Carefully avoiding the unpleasant truth that this was exactly what I'd been thinking just before I had first kissed Nicholas, I yanked on my sandals, pulling the straps as tight as they would go. Yet again, my only underwear was drying in the bathroom, so I put on the snuggest of my borrowed tops, with a longer-sleeved one over it, and a pair of cotton shorts. Then I strode out of my bedroom, my sandals flapping with every step.

Realizing that it was still fairly dark, I wondered briefly whether doing an indoor gym session might be a more prudent idea than venturing outdoors into an area where one of the Big Five species roamed—albeit a timid one. Where had Nicholas said the gym was? In the east wing? That would be on the opposite side of the house from his bedroom.

I walked quietly down the corridor, and to my surprise I heard the sounds coming from the gym long before I reached the door.

The squeak of trainers on a polished floor. A series of hard, smacking thuds.

Grunts and rapid breaths, indicating somebody was doing an intensive session.

It could only be Nicholas—but what equipment was he using to make that noise?

I tiptoed to the doorway and peeked round the open door.

The gym was a big, airy space with white walls and equipment arranged neatly around its perimeter. Just one light was turned on—a low-wattage lamp by the entrance desk—but despite its weak, orange glow, there was enough light for me to see the details of what was happening inside.

Wearing only a pair of trainers, a pair of well used boxing gloves, and the dark shorts I'd seen him in last night, Nicholas was working out on a piece of equipment that he hadn't told me about. It hung in the center of the room—a heavy, red punching bag.

He had his back to me and he was battering it with vicious force, snapping out a series of lethal-looking punches before stepping back, rebalancing, and launching some powerful roundhouse kicks. Then, closing in, he bludgeoned the bag once again. His muscles were coiled and bulky under his sweat-soaked skin and he was panting for breath. The kicks and punches he was throwing looked so hard and brutal that if they had landed on a live opponent, I did not doubt they would have done serious damage.

Even though the powerful movements were hypnotic to watch, I felt as if I was intruding on his privacy by standing here and looking in. The focused fury of this workout felt somehow personal. I thought this was more than just fitness training. It was as if he was revealing a side of himself in the gym that he'd never shown to me before. An angry side, that sent a shudder of fear through me.

As he attacked the bag yet again, putting all his weight behind the blows, I could hear his breathing coming in tortured gasps. He was pushing himself to his limits with this workout. I had the feeling that at this moment, Nicholas was existing in a private world of his own making—a world where he was being forced to fight for his life, or for his sanity. I thought that even if he were to move round to face me, he might not notice me.

Finally, I tore my eyes away. I retreated as silently as I'd arrived, but as I walked back down the passage, a tortured cry stopped me in my tracks. Ragged sobbing followed.

Holding my breath, I tiptoed back to the doorway to see Nicholas slung over the punching bag, his shoulders shaking as he cried like a baby.

The sight made my heart contract. I longed to comfort him, to put my arms around him, to soothe his deep pain even though I could not understand it. But I couldn't. Instead, I turned away and crept back through the house to the front door. I unlocked it and stepped outside into the morning which, though still cool, had now turned from dark to grey.

An hour later, I returned to the house at a slow jog, having walked the entire track. My legs were pleasantly tired, my feet in their inappropriate shoes felt sore, but thanks to the exercise I felt as if I'd finally achieved some much-needed mental balance. Plus, I'd encountered a herd of impala behind a stand of thorn bushes who hadn't noticed me until I'd been a few yards away. Amazed and laughing, I'd watched as they'd snorted in panic at sensing my presence and, a moment later, the small herd had hightailed it through the scrubby grass.

On my way up to the house, I stopped to admire a colorful tree with a wide canopy of branches covered in red-gold blossoms. This must be a coral tree, I decided—I'd read about them in one of the brochures at Kevin's and Byron's hotel. Peering more closely, I was charmed to notice a stick insect crawling along one of the smaller branches. He was so well camouflaged that I'd never have seen him if I hadn't spied the movement. His body looked exactly like a long, thin twig. Even his legs looked like miniature sticks. Gazing past him, I caught my breath at the beauty of the view—the muted greens and greys of the landscape still shrouded in mist while, on the horizon, the edges of the scattered clouds were turning golden. It was so peaceful and yet so wild. I longed for my camera. I wanted to capture a close-up of that insect among those coral blossoms, with the glowing sky as a backdrop.

Reluctantly, I turned away from the magical sight. As I walked up to the front door it opened, and I stopped in my tracks when I saw Nicholas in the doorway, his face hard. His hair was still wet from the shower and he was wearing a khaki shirt and shorts. My heart barely had time to skip a beat at the sight of his presence before I saw that in his right hand he held a long and lethal-looking Remington.

"Erin. I've been looking for you."

"With that gun?" After seeing him forcing himself through that punishing workout, and now carrying a firearm, I was unsure what his motives might be.

His lips softened into a reluctant smile at my words, and with that, I saw the Nicholas I knew return. "I wanted to tell you I'm going to repair the boundary fence, so you'll be on your own here until Miriam arrives and I'd like you to keep the doors locked until then."

"That's no problem. How do you know the fence is broken?"

"Game rangers in Kruger Park were patrolling and they called me a few minutes ago to say the wires looked slack. They can't get through to see what the problem is because the tracks on their side are still too deep under water."

"When you say broken, do you mean it's damaged to the extent that all the elephants and lions could get through?" Visions of my walk having turned into an involuntary race for my life flashed through my mind.

"Yes. They could already be roaming in this secure area. And, more seriously, poachers could gain access. In fact, the fence could have been damaged by poachers. The rangers said they heard shooting in the park last night. These criminals are always heavily armed and extremely dangerous. So I need to go and sort it out urgently."

"Thus the gun?"

"It's a safety precaution. A very necessary one, I'm afraid."

"Are you going on your own?"

"I am."

"Do you need a hand?" The minute I'd said the words, I could have kicked myself. Why did I keep doing this? What was it that made me continually seek out the company of this self-confessed womanizer, despite my own stern warnings to myself not to?

"I'd appreciate some help. It's likely to be hard work, though."

"I'm not afraid of that."

He glanced at the pale pink, cloudless sky. "And hot work, too. Bring a hat with you, and sunscreen. I'll see you out by the car."

Without waiting for an answer, Nicholas turned and strode in the direction of the garage, pausing only to pick up a thermos flask and a bottle of water from the kitchen counter.

I was ready in a couple of minutes, sunscreen liberally slathered over my skin. I climbed into the passenger seat of the Land Cruiser and we set off, following the paved driveway for a few hundred yards before turning left and joining a bumpy dirt track that wound its way deep into the bush.

"Where's Joshua this morning?" I asked.

"Joshua and his team have already left to start sandbagging the river bank. If they get enough done today, the new bridge could be started tomorrow."

Tomorrow? So soon?

He glanced at me and I hastily arranged my features into a smile. "That's great news. Let's hope it all goes well."

Inside, though, I couldn't help feeling a stab of disappointment.

"And I had a message from another farmer that your hired car was washed up near a ravine twenty miles south of here. I've notified the police. If they can get to it safely—which is doubtful—they'll be able to see if there is any salvageable equipment inside. If not, they'll at least be able to take photos."

"That will be helpful. The insurance company has been asking for proof of the accident."

Thinking again of that rainy afternoon, I couldn't help but imagine what would have happened if I had been trapped inside… if Nicholas had not been in time to save me before the powerful force of the water had sent the car bobbing into the center, pulled downstream by the rushing water.

They would have been looking for my body now. Unsalvageable for sure.

I shivered, staring ahead at the rolling hills, and perhaps Nicholas sensed my discomfort, because he said, "So, if the bridge hadn't been washed away, what would you be doing now?"

Grateful for the distraction, I told him, "I'd be staying in the Royal Africa Hotel. Which, I think, is an hour's drive from here."

"The Royal Africa? That's a premium place. The owner, Hennie Pretorius, is an acquaintance of mine. It's more like an hour and a half away, though. Much further south."

"An acquaintance of yours?" Fear stabbed me again. "Nicholas, in case Vince asks, would you mind…"

He sighed. "Would I mind phoning Hennie and asking him not to mention me to your husband?"

"Yes."

Without further argument, he took out his phone and dialed.

"Hey, Hennie, Nick here," he said. "Yes, all's good. I'm phoning about a guest who's staying with you now. Vince Mitchell, a photographer from New York."

He waited, listened, smiled. "Difficult customer? That doesn't surprise me. Listen, I've got his wife staying at my lodge. She was stranded here when the river flooded." There was another pause, and then he laughed. "Very lucky?" he said. "Yes, yes, as always. Do me a favor. Don't mention me to Vince Mitchell. And if he asks you, tell him I'm married."

I could hear Hennie laughing, too, before Nicholas disconnected.

"Thank you," I said.

Nicholas put his phone away.

"So, back to my original question. What would you be doing now if you hadn't been stranded here?" he asked.

"Since it's just before dawn, I'd more than likely be out shooting."

"Hoping to photograph the Big Five?"

"Some shots of them would be great," I agreed, "but that's not what we traveled here to do. Vince was booked for a *Vogue* fashion shoot in a safari setting. And, to be honest, although I've done whatever pays the bills in the past, my forte is more on the creative side than on larger wildlife. Colors, shapes. An unusual flower. An insect going about his business. Cloud formations just before a storm."

Nicholas nodded. "I like the sound of that. That's seeing nature as it really is… that's what it's all about. More so than just capturing the biggest and the fiercest."

"What would you be doing now?" I asked him. "Out in the bush, shooting? Just like me except with a gun instead of a camera?"

"No. I'm not a hunter."

"You're not?"

"I can shoot, but I don't hunt for fun. I've used this gun a few times in the past here, each time to put an injured animal out of its pain. So, no, Erin, I wouldn't be in the bush. In fact, I wouldn't even be here. Yesterday I had three meetings lined up in Nelspruit, followed by a flight to Johannesburg and another four meetings there. And after that I was going to fly to Somalia."

"To Somalia?" I stared at him, incredulous. "Isn't that very dangerous right now?"

Nicholas shrugged. "I was going to do a two week shift with Doctors without Borders, running an emergency medical center there while the resident medic took leave. I used to work for Doctors without Borders full time at one stage. I still like to do the occasional shift."

"And all the meetings?"

"Those were business meetings."

Business? Why didn't he want to give me any other details?

"You're a puzzling man, Nicholas," I remarked after a short pause.

"I don't try to be."

"Is that another wildebeest beyond that bush?"

He leaned across. "I can't see one. Oh, wait. Yes, I can. There he is. You really are incredibly sharp-eyed, Erin."

Through a gap in the branches of the bushes beyond where the wildebeest grazed I caught sight of the rising sun—a crimson orb laced with filigree clouds. Oh, for a camera; to try and capture this suffusion of color, and the twisted, unique silhouettes of the trees that framed it.

"I'm interested to know where you come from," I told Nicholas, tearing my eyes away from the incredible sight. "What made you who you are. And—it's a personal question, I know—but how did you end up here, after being a paramedic?"

He glanced at me, amusement in his eyes. "You mean how I could afford to buy the place?"

"Well, yes."

"Family money," he said, and in his words I heard distaste. "And as for where I come from and what has made me who I am… that's not something I like to talk about."

"Oh," I said, nonplussed.

"Tell me about yourself, rather. How you came to be a photographer." He slowed the car to ease it over a deep rut in the road.

"I've always been artistic," I admitted. "I'm a creative person. Ask me to do math and I couldn't to save my life. But ask me to describe this sunset—to capture it with my camera and try to produce an image which holds the essence of these colors… these pinks and ochers and mauves and reds, how perfectly they blend, the wildness of them, this incredible quality of clearness to the air—well, I could be here all day talking to you."

"I can relate to that." Nicholas's voice was soft.

"I grew up in Florida—my mother still lives there. I had a little brother, but he died when I was a teenager." I let out a long breath and turned my face away.

"I'm so sorry to hear that," Nicholas said gently.

"I studied photography. Then I traveled all over the States, working wherever I went. Sometimes in my profession, other times doing whatever came along."

"Interesting," he observed. "Where did you go?"

"I've lived in—let me think, now—Port Saint Lucie, Charlotte, Detroit, Kansas City, Dayton, a few places in California, a couple of places in New Jersey, and most recently New York City. Usually for a few months before moving on. Never more than a year or so in any one place."

"Why is that?"

"It's not something I talk about," I shot back.

The car crested a hill and on the steep downhill on the other side, the bush thinned out, with trees becoming taller and interspersed with green-gold grassland. Ahead of us ran the silvery stretch of the fence line. This fence would have done justice to a high-security prison. It was about ten feet high, and made not only of fine wire but also of thick steel cabling strung tightly between tall and sturdy metal posts which were embedded in a solid-looking concrete base.

"The fine wires are usually electrified," Nicholas said, "either by mains or generator. It's only in the past two days this fence had been without power."

But now, looking more carefully, I noticed a stretch of wires near the base of the fence hung loosely. There was definitely damage, and I found my stomach tensing at the likelihood that criminals had tampered with the fence.

"Have you had poachers gain access before?" I asked him.

He nodded grimly. "Once. Last year."

"And what happened?"

His lips tightened. "They shot two of my rhino. Killed one, injured the other, dehorned both of them. We tracked them through the park and the police arrested them before they managed to escape with the horns."

"Oh, no, that is terrible."

"Since then, the fence has been kept electrified. Even if they try to breach it, the alarm should sound, but there's always the danger they know how to bypass it."

We climbed out of the car and walked slowly toward the boundary. Birds were twittering all around me and the trill of the cicadas rang in my ears. The day was already warm and from somewhere nearby I could hear the rippling of water. Looking more closely, I saw a small stream flowed through the fence, and that the grasses and bush surrounding it looked flattened as if they had been swept by floodwater. An area in front of the concrete had been severely eroded by the water, although it looked as if the concrete base itself, which must be more than a yard deep, had not been damaged.

"That's what caused the break," Nicholas observed, pointing.

A little further on, a fallen tree had been swept into the fence. Its tough, gnarled branches had caught and pulled the finer wires, the force causing them to snap. The cables had held it, though, and now it lay, pinned against the fence, its branches tangled in the wires.

"The tree broke the fence. But there have been people around here since then. Look."

I shivered as I saw the evidence in the muddy soil. These were not animal tracks, they were human footprints, and to my untrained eye it looked like more than one person had climbed through the gap.

"They might have gone back again," Nicholas muttered, bending to examine the prints closely. "If they're on this side, they won't be showing themselves now; they'll be hiding out somewhere safe until dark. Either way, we need to fix this damage. How are your wood-working skills, Erin? We'll have to cut this up to get it out, and while I'm here, I want to fill in that eroded area as well."

"I'm handy with a saw," I told him. "And a shovel. When I was living in Detroit in winter, I shared a house with three other girls, and I was always the designated snow shoveler."

"You can start with that, then."

Returning to the car, he opened the boot, and took out a shiny yellow steel shovel, which he handed to me along with a brand new pair of gardening gloves. He then removed an axe and a saw.

"Oh, for battery-operated power tools," I quipped.

"I have plenty, but they're all in use down at the river," Nicholas told me with a grin.

Two hard-working hours later, the job was done. The tree had been chopped up and its branches removed by Nicholas, who'd then repaired the wires. Finally, he'd grabbed another spade and helped me with the job of filling in the last of the eroded section.

The sun was higher in the sky now. My throat felt parched and I was streaming with sweat. My dark hair was sodden and I wished I hadn't worn a white top, because it was so wet that my breasts were clearly visible. My muscles were burning. This had been hard physical work and I knew I would sleep well tonight.

"Well done." Nicholas wiped sweat from his own forehead. His gaze roamed over me, taking in my nearly-transparent T-shirt, before he bent to pick up the tools and take them back to the car.

The water he'd brought with him was still cold. I drank gratefully from the bottle and then Nicholas handed me the cup from the thermos flask, which I was delighted to discover was brimming with more of the icy, sweet lemonade we'd had last night.

"I need a shower," I told him when we'd both drunk our fill.

"I can help you there," he said. "Come this way."

He leaned into the back of the car, picked up his rifle, and removed two towels before heading in the direction of the steep hill we'd driven down when we arrived. Curious, I followed him. He walked round the side of the hill toward a high rocky outcrop which formed a cliff. The sound of the water was even louder here, and as we rounded the corner, I saw that the stream flowed over the cliff itself, creating a miniature waterfall, before disappearing into the grasses below.

The rock where I was standing was smooth and cool. I kicked off my shoes and stepped under the falling stream. The water was crystal clear and surprisingly chilly, as if it came from deep underground—the coldness took my breath away for a moment before it became exhilarating. The water drummed down on my head and shoulders, soaked my hair, sluiced through the light clothing I wore. I turned my face up to it, spread my arms and let it splash over my aching muscles, cooling and soothing them.

Another minute and the cold became too much to bear. I stepped away, shivering, as Nicholas took my place. He'd propped his rifle against the base of the cliff and laid the towels out on a flat ledge of rock in the sun, which right then didn't feel very warm at all. My clothing was streaming with water and for a moment I considered taking it off and squeezing it out—but then prudence won over.

Even so, as I sat down on the towel, shivering, with my arms wrapped around me, I was filled with a sudden sense of unreality. Here I was, alive and well, but trapped in an alternate existence. It was as if the accident had pulled me out of my old life, and plunged me into a new one.

"And whose fault had the accident been?" a tiny voice whispered inside me.

Of course, nobody could have known that the floods would destroy the bridge. But it was Vince who'd decreed that the two of us should travel apart. Riding high himself in the terrain-appropriate Land Rover, he'd ordered me to climb inside a far less suitable car, to drive in terrible weather conditions and with a driver whom we barely knew, who'd taken the job only the day before.

And all because of what? His own delusional and illogical jealousy. It was strange how when I was with Vince, I'd gone to such lengths to try and defuse this. Insisting I loved him, managing my own behavior, trying to avoid situations where this might occur. I'd been so stubbornly focused on keeping things from going wrong that I'd never allowed myself to feel the anger I was starting to feel now.

How could he object to me being friendly with a happily married homosexual man, but then order me to get in a car with a young and unknown stranger? Or was that something that, at some stage in the future, he would have used against me, too?

And then, when the accident occurred, he'd been driving too far ahead of us to realize the fact. Angry at the wrong road he'd taken, his ego bruised by our pointless journey through the rainy bushveld, he'd crossed the bridge at least twenty minutes ahead of us... and although it had been starting to flood at that stage, Vince hadn't stopped.

He hadn't waited.

At that crucial time, he had not cared.

One thing was for sure—although fate had played a role, the fact that I'd ended up here had been in no way my own fault. And, with a sudden hardening of my resolve, I decided I was going to refuse to feel guilty about anything that I did while I was here.

These few days were the beginning of the rest of my life—a life that I would not have been living now if Nicholas had not rescued me. They could be regarded as a blessing—a magical time that I would never, ever enjoy again.

And, right then, I decided I was going to spend them in whatever way made me happy.

CHAPTER 12

A SPLASHY THUD STARTLED me from my reverie. It was Nicholas's shirt, soaking wet from the waterfall, which he'd tossed onto the warm rock nearby. I couldn't help but stare at the sight of him, clad only in his khaki shorts, the water cascading down over his broad shoulders and those muscular, defined arms.

God, he was beautiful, and I felt a pang of jealousy as I thought of Angela the Australian journalist, and of all the other women with whom he'd consorted over the years.

He stepped out from under the waterfall and came to sit beside me.

"It's refreshing, isn't it?"

"It's freezing," I laughed. His proximity to me was doing it again. I was aware of every inch of my body, and of his. The droplets of water trickled down his tanned skin, sparkling in the sun. His arm was so close to mine that we almost brushed. I remembered how he'd touched me, pleasured me, so intimately the previous day. Now the intensity of my desire for him made me feel ill.

My own angry thoughts earlier had made me rebellious, and the hard physical work had tired me, broken down the barriers I'd been working so hard to keep in place. Now all that was left was honesty—the raw truth of my own shameful longing.

The heat had already ratcheted up again. The sun was beating down onto my shirt, now warmer but still damp. It was reflecting off every brilliant drop from the waterfall. I half turned to him as I spoke.

Then I did what I had been longing to do. I lifted my arm and stroked my fingers over his shoulder, feeling the skin, smooth and still cool, and the ripped definition beneath. I ran my fingertips down his back, over the ridges of muscle on either side of his spine.

His eyes widened at the touch. His pale blue gaze burned mine, his face just inches away from my own. In his expression I saw the same helpless lust that had me in its grip.

"I've reconsidered your offer," I whispered.

His kiss stopped my words.

His lips parted to taste my own as he let out an audible groan. My lips softened, yielding to his. Warm and slick, his tongue found mine, sliding against my own in a way that had my pulse suddenly racing. His hands roamed over my back, trailing lower to slip under the waistband of my pants and caress my buttocks.

In that moment I was lost in eternity. God, I could have kissed him forever; it was the purest, most erotic sensory bliss—but it was triggering a need that was driving me wild—and him, too.

With hungry fingers he tugged at my pants, pulling them down, easing them off, his touch warm against my own flesh. And I helped him, kicking my discarded clothing to one side even as he yanked his own shorts down to free his substantial erection.

He grasped me around my waist, pulled me onto his thighs so that we were sitting, my legs straddling his. His breathing was rapid, matching my own. With a groan he cupped his hands around my buttocks, pulling me closer so that our bodies were tight against each other. He kissed me again, slowly and lusciously, and I kissed him back, my body welded to his.

I could feel his cock, thick and hard, pressing against the lips of my naked sex. This was all too raw, too sudden, far too dangerous… but I had no more chance of stopping than I did of flying.

As if he'd read my mind, he broke the kiss.

"You are far too sexy." His hands stroked my hair, his fingers smoothing over the dampened strands. "You're driving me crazy. I've been feeling as if I'm sixteen again, carrying this damned condom round with me day and night. Never believing I'd have the chance to use it."

"I touched myself last night thinking of you," I whispered, and saw his eyes widen in amazement at my words.

"God, Erin," he choked out. "That's such a turn-on. You have no idea what you're doing to me…"

Swiftly, he fumbled for his discarded shorts and pulled a foil wrapper from the back pocket. He tore the wrapper open, rolled it on.

This was my last opportunity to say no… the final chance to stop this. Instead I was kneeling over him, clutching his broad shoulders, just about panting with desire as his fingers moved between my legs and traced circles of pleasure over my swollen lips before slipping inside.

"You're so ready, so wet. You're so needy to be fucked." His voice was husky.

"So do it," I whispered. His words were making me feel reckless and dizzy with lust. His fingering had turned me molten, liquid. I wanted to melt into him.

I reached down and grasped his thick shaft, feeling his heat, his hardness under the slick, stretched latex. His breathing quickened as I guided him to the place where his fingers had so recently pleasured. I was so hungry for him; there was a throbbing need deep inside me that I was desperate for him to fill.

His cock gently touched the delicate flesh at my entrance, a sensual, inviting caress that had me moaning in anticipation of what was to follow. I moved my hips and his head eased inside me, pushing my swollen lips apart. I let out an involuntary gasp at the exquisite stretching sensation, as the nerve endings at my entrance pulsed with pleasure.

Nicholas was breathing fast, staring into my eyes, his handsome face rigid with desire. His gaze was consuming me and at that moment, I knew he was as much of a slave to his body's needs as I was to mine.

I pushed down, taking him deeper inside me, catching my breath at the unexpected size of him. He was big… big everywhere, from his height and the width of his shoulders to his broad, square hands and the thick hardness of his cock. It felt so sexy to be stretched and opened by him. This was more than erotic… it was possession.

I felt myself tauten with delight and from the breathy groan he uttered, I knew he had felt me, too. His hands closed over my thighs, easing me all the way down onto him as he arched his hips to meet me.

I let out a small moan as he buried himself to the hilt inside me. The sense of fullness was incredible, causing my breath to come in shallow gasps. My brain was whirling at the enormity of what I was doing with this man, this philanderer who'd made his disreputable intentions clear at the first opportunity. There was no going back now, no denying what we were doing. He was having his way with me, using me just like every other one of the slutty women he'd smooth talked into bed… this wasn't lovemaking. It was fucking. His cock was all the way in me… oh God, but why did it feel so good? I was quivering, throbbing with the intensity of my desire.

"It's okay, Erin" he murmured, as if sensing my thoughts. "It's all right to let yourself feel pleasure." His face was open with lust, his features slack, and staring at him made me think of a fallen saint.

His hips rocked rhythmically under me, opening me fully to him with his deep, strong thrusts. Then, grasping my buttocks, he angled himself into me, rubbing over a sweet spot so responsive that it sent liquid fire coursing through me. I started jerking involuntarily toward him in reaction to this, my body a puppet on his strings, and he groaned.

"That's good," he murmured. His fingers stroked my breasts, feeling my nipples erect and defined through the fine, damp fabric of my blouse. He squeezed them between his fingers and thumbs, then rubbed his fingertips over them, pinching them gently, and my mouth opened at the intense sensual gratification this offered.

"You like it?" he whispered. "You want more?"

His skin was hot, slick, beaded with the same perspiration that was trickling down my body, out here, thanks to the furnace of the morning and the extremes of our lust.

He squeezed my nipples again, in rhythm with the thrusts of his cock, then as he pushed harder inside me, began rubbing his fingers over them rapidly. The liquid delight of his touch coursed deeply and powerfully through me, igniting every cell of my body. The friction of his thick cock inside me caused me to shudder… a sensation which became too sweet to bear. I could feel myself coiling and tightening around him. My heart was banging as I gasped for air.

"I'm… oh, yes, I'm…"

With a hot rush of delight, I came, crying out in amazement at the intensity of the release. I dug my fingers into his solid biceps, squeezing him hard, shuddering as the waves of my orgasm causing me to jerk and writhe.

He grasped my buttocks, his hands digging into my flesh as he thrust, hard and rapidly, before letting out an explosive cry and pulling me down toward him.

"Ah, God, Erin."

Plastered against his body, clamped to him by his urgent hands, my rough breathing matched his own. I felt his hips powerfully convulse, and the deep, strong pulses of his release inside me.

I lay on top of Nicholas, his grip holding me close. I could still feel him inside me, could feel the pounding of his heart and the rapid rise and fall of his chest. As reality filtered in once more, I became aware of the sounds around us. The splashing of water, the trill of the cicadas, the occasional bird call from the nearby trees.

The boiling heat of the sun, now higher in the sky.

After a while, his grasp relaxed and I sat up, then climbed carefully off him and stood on legs that felt surprisingly weak. My shorts, still damp but now warm, were lying discarded near the cliff. Feeling suddenly self-conscious about being outside in the open, even though I knew we were in the middle of nowhere on Nicholas's private land, I pulled them on.

Nicholas walked to the car—to dispose of the condom, I assumed. I watched him as he returned, picked his clothes up and got dressed.

I didn't know what to say. I knew I should feel cheap and guilty—and I did—but it did not alter the truth of my attraction to him. The physical tug was so strong it made me want to hold him now. To push his tousled hair back from his face and smooth the creases out of his rumpled shirt. To bury my face in his neck and inhale his musky, masculine scent.

Be strong, I told myself, turning away to survey the bushveld. Don't cross the line between fucking and intimacy. You can't let yourself become entangled with him. What you're enjoying now is pure physical indulgence. You're using him just as he's using you. This is fucking. It's your weakness, revenge, celebration of survival, however you want to try and justify it. Whatever, it's certainly nothing to be proud of.

And yet, my body had never felt more blissfully satiated in my life. Not with any other lover... not even with Vince.

Nicholas walked toward me and I braced myself to resist his touch in the unlikely event that he offered it.

And then I caught my breath as, only a few yards away, the tiniest and most perfectly formed antelope I had ever seen, standing just a little over two feet high, picked its way delicately through the long grass before leaping onto a low shelf of rock.

His hand grasped mine and, forgetting my promise to myself, I held it tightly. We both stood still as we watched and a smile of pure wonderment spread over my face.

"It's so beautiful," I breathed, and even at that sound the animal's large ears flicked. "Is it a baby?"

"No," he whispered back. "Fully grown."

We watched as, with another trotting jump, it soundlessly crossed the rock and vanished once again into the long grass.

"It's a steenbok," Nicholas told me, still speaking in a low voice. "One of the very smallest antelope. I didn't even know there were any in this part of the estate. There were none listed in the inventory." Glancing at him I saw my own delight reflected in his eyes.

"I guess you got a small buck bonus," I joked, and he laughed, smoothing my hair—which was now in a state somewhere between tangled and dreadlocked—back from my face.

"I guess I did."

Five minutes later we were in the car and heading back to the lodge, with the air conditioning on full blast and slowly starting to cool down and banish the oppressive heat.

"So you don't know exactly what animals are in this section of your park," I observed.

"Well, I thought I did. They were listed in detail, but there are supposed to be two red hartebeest in here that I've never managed to spot, and there are more eland than were listed, as well as that little steenbok."

"What made you buy this place? Did you live in the area previously?"

"No. I like space and solitude, though, and this offered both at a time I needed it. I've lived…" He tightened his lips as if aware he was telling me too much, but unwilling to stop. "I've lived in Johannesburg, Cape Town, London, and Zurich, mostly. Those are the cities where I grew up. Then I've worked in a lot of other, less civilized places in my capacity as a paramedic. Ivory Coast. Sri Lanka. Afghanistan. Sometimes for weeks, sometimes for months."

He stopped speaking but didn't look at me, instead staring ahead as the grass-lined track unrolled in front of us.

"And your family? Where are they now?"

Nicholas shrugged, the gesture at once defensive and angry. "Erin, it doesn't matter. And it doesn't concern you."

"Well, all right, then," I shot back, unreasonably hurt by this dismissal. "Like you said, I'm here for a week, then I'm gone. Now I've fucked you, which I'll probably regret, but I'll do it again if and when I feel like it. Apart from that, you're right. I shouldn't give a shit about you."

I stared angrily out of the passenger window. Not even the sight of three energetically cantering zebra could bring a smile to my face.

"I'm sorry," Nicholas said after a while. I glanced at him. Was it my imagination, or did he look rather hurt by my callous words?

"Whatever." I was still smoldering, unwilling to accept his apology.

"I'm not used to being asked that kind of question." The car's tires rolled onto smooth paving as we drove up the driveway.

Now I swung round to face him. "Nicholas, that kind of question is perfectly normal. In fact, I was just trying to make polite conversation when you went all weird on me. Jeez, what the hell's a safe topic around you apart from wildlife?"

"Almost anything. Books, art, music, current events. You name it. As long as the topic isn't Nicholas de Lanoy, I'm happy."

"I'll certainly bear that in mind in the future." He parked in the garage and I opened the door, planted my feet on the ground, and then on impulse, leaned back in. "And I would like you to know that you don't have a monopoly on fucked-up family life. You're not the only one. So, for your information, Erin Mitchell is also off-limits as a conversation topic from now on."

I slammed the door behind me and stomped out of the garage into the cool, airy lodge.

CHAPTER 13

I WAS HALFWAY DOWN the corridor leading to my bedroom when I realized that the lodge was not just cool, but deliciously cold. Music was playing from the dining room and I could hear the sound of a vacuum cleaner coming from somewhere nearby.

I entered my bedroom to find Miriam folding a small pile of freshly laundered clothes and towels into the cupboard.

"Good morning," she said cheerfully, seeming not to notice my disheveled appearance or, more probably, simply accustomed to women looking the way I did when they'd spent some time in the company of her boss.

"Morning," I responded with a tight smile.

"We have full power again. The main supply is restored," she told me.

"Oh, that's great."

"It is, yes. We were lucky. The damage was not on this side of the river. The storm knocked a transformer out on the other side, so they were able to repair it this morning. I will bring coffee now. And would you like a waffle? Ice cream and fruit salad?"

"Thanks," I told her. It was easier not to resist Miriam when she'd made her mind up. In that respect, I had to admit, she had something in common with her employer.

After she'd left the room I stepped under the shower to wash and condition my hair. When I stood under the hot water I thought I could smell Nicholas on me, and I felt both cheap and promiscuous as I poured half the bottle of shower gel into my hands to banish his scent from my skin. I soaped my sensitive breasts, and washed between my legs, where I was still swollen and slick from the sex we'd had.

My body was a mess of bruises. The one on my chest was looking worse every day—a grim thunderstorm landscape of purples and yellows. It was tender to the touch, but looked worse than it felt. Others, too. A small bruise on my upper thigh and one on my calf.

And, on the inside of my left arm, the incriminating line of blue-black fingerprints from where Vince had grabbed me. Those, also, were at their worst now. Another few days and I hoped they would fade, together with the giant bruise on my hipbone, now purple, red, and yellow, from where I'd fallen against the corner of the desk when he'd yanked me toward him.

Back in the bedroom, wearing clean clothes and with my hair finally combed out and under control again, I devoured the large, late breakfast, which Miriam had left on the table. I was surprised by my appetite until I remembered what a physically active morning it had been.

I turned my phone on.

Waiting to see if I had a message from Vince, I felt acute nausea. What would I tell him? How would I word my story? Would he be able to pick up from my voice what I had done?

There was no message although the network notified me I'd had three missed calls from him since my phone had been off. I called him, praying he wouldn't answer, and he didn't. I left a brief message, telling him I hoped his shoot was going well and that I loved him. I felt sick while I was saying the words. Would the rest of my marriage feel like this—as if I was living a lie?

I turned my phone off again and connected to the Internet to find I had mail. The insurance company had sent a claim form for me to fill in, and Samantha had messaged me again.

Hey, girlfriend… Sam's mail read. *I haven't heard back from you since my last mail. What's going on? Are you sure you're okay? Please write soon… I'm worried. Love and hugs.*

Reading her words made me smile.

I took a little while to compose a reply.

Hey girlfriend yourself!

I'm sorry about the lack of communication. I didn't know how best to reply to your last mail. I was hoping if I waited a day or two, everything would be sorted out and I could tell you it was all fine. But instead, it's all gotten much more complicated. It's only since I've been apart from Vince that I've had a chance to realize how crazy jealous he can be. And that's not even the worst of it.

I paused for a moment, thinking what my next words should be.

I've just been unfaithful to Vince with the man who saved me from drowning, the one I told you about, who owns this estate and who's a serial womanizer. I don't know how I feel now or what to do. I feel very alone. I've made some stupid decisions and I think they might have started further back than this morning. My life is a mess at the moment and I don't know how to fix it.

I stared down at the words on the screen.

This was a confession. It was dangerous.

Please, please don't tell Vince any of this. Strictest secrecy, okay?

This email could get me into big trouble. I should delete it or at the very least, make it less incriminating. In the end, I didn't. Before I could change my mind, I pressed send. I watched it go, feeling so tense that when there was a knock on my bedroom door, I almost jumped out of my skin.

"Who—who is it?" I fumbled with the mouse, clicked the window closed.

"It's me. Nick."

Nick?

"What is it?" And then, realizing the idiocy of conducting a conversation with him through a closed door, I added, "Come in."

He opened the door and walked in. He, too, looked freshly showered. His damp hair was the color of honey and he was wearing a smart white golf shirt with the leopard logo I now recognized. I could see fine golden hairs on his bronzed forearms. I wanted to touch him. I craved the feeling of his skin under my fingertips. I knew exactly what it would be like—a little warmer than my own and surprisingly silken to the touch.

I shook my head briefly, hoping to clear these dangerous, intruding thoughts.

"Sit down," I said, and he took a seat on the armchair nearby.

"Much more pleasant in here with the A.C. operational," he observed. "Anyway, I came to tell you we've been invited to a party."

"A party?" I frowned at him, confused. "Both of us? Who…?"

"It's to celebrate the electricity being reconnected, apparently." I realized Nicholas looked as perplexed by this invitation as I felt. "Thandiwe and Berndt are holding it—the owners of the estate where we went yesterday, remember? They've invited everyone on this side of the river; a total of seven households, including ours."

"Well, we'd better be polite and go, then."

"I suppose so." He gave me a baffled smile. "This is a new one for me. Socializing with all the neighbors."

I couldn't help feeling amused that, finally, I'd found an area where Nicholas felt out of his depth. Saving people's lives and starting up businesses were clearly all in a day's work for him, but attending a local get-together was not.

Or perhaps that wasn't what was troubling him. Suddenly, I thought of the reason why he might have come to tell me this.

"Listen, if you'd rather I didn't go with you, I'll be totally fine staying here."

Two deep furrows appeared in his brow. "How do you mean?"

"Well…" Damn. I'd misunderstood him and now I was fumbling to get my point across. "We hardly know each other, and these are your neighbors. You might want to socialize with them without having a—well, without me around."

"I see what you were trying to say." He was silent for a moment. "Erin, can I tell you something?"

"Sure."

"I really enjoy your company. I want you to come along with me. If you're wondering whether the neighbors know what I'm like, and whose company I've enjoyed in the past, and what they'll be thinking about you, all I can tell you is that they don't know. And it's not as if I've had multiple liaisons recently in any case. The last time I slept with anybody was with Angela."

"With Angela?" But that had been nearly six months ago.

"Yes."

"Oh." I was quiet for a minute. "You've been misrepresenting yourself to me then. Here I was thinking you had a different partner every two weeks."

The shadow of a smile warmed his face. "A decade ago, you would have been about right with that guess. Nowadays, I'm more selective. I apologize for the misrepresentation."

"Accepted." Despite all my efforts not to, I was smiling, too. "I'll go to the party with you. What time do we have to be ready, and is there anything we need to bring?"

"Bring?" He stared at me, nonplussed. "Damn it. I forgot to ask. I'd better call Thandiwe back."

"Ask her if she needs a salad. Or…" What else had I seen in the fridge? "Or a fruit salad. We could take both. And we should bring drinks, of course."

"Drinks, yes." Still frowning, he took his phone out of his pocket and dialed her number.

※ ※ ※

By six-thirty p.m. we were ready to go. I was wearing the only dress in my collection of borrowed clothes—a silken sundress—and over it, to cover the bruises on my arm, a light, white lace jersey that was a size too big. The green salad, which I had made, and a fruit salad made by Miriam were packed in the cooler box, together with a six-pack of beer, wine, and a bottle of champagne. Behind us, Joshua and Miriam, who had also been invited, were climbing into the beige estate vehicle.

The evening was finally starting to cool down and clouds were boiling on the eastern horizon. Wind tugged at the tree branches.

"More rain on the way," Nicholas observed. "I hope this doesn't wash away the sandbags Joshua spent all day packing in."

"I hope it doesn't take the power box out again, otherwise they'll have to cancel the party," I added, causing Nicholas to raise his eyebrows.

"Let's hope it doesn't."

When we arrived at the estate, five other large vehicles were already parked in the driveway. Music was blaring from loudspeakers set up in the covered outdoor entertainment area. A string of colored lights had been threaded along the top of the patio roof.

"Good evening!" Thandiwe, resplendent in a brightly patterned gown, bustled over to greet us all, and gave me a hug. "Thank you for coming, and for bringing the salads. Erin, they've made good progress with the river banks today. I'm sure it won't be long before you're back with your hubby, but in the meantime we're so glad to have you here."

I didn't dare look at Nicholas as she spoke. Then she turned to him. "Evening, Doctor! Lovely to see you. David's chin is much better. He's playing upstairs now." She kissed him on the cheek, then gestured toward the party lights. "Please go and enjoy yourselves. I apologize for the loud music. When you have fourteen-year-old and twelve-year-old girls, these things just happen!"

Nicholas and I walked toward the entertainment area, but Thandiwe tugged at my arm and held me back.

"I thought I'd just let you know," she said in a stage whisper. "The Groenewalds, who live on the farm to the north of us, have their niece visiting. She's twenty-three and gorgeous! They want to set her up with Nicholas. Isn't that exciting? I'm going to introduce him to her now. There may be some matchmaking happening here tonight." She gave me a conspiratorial grin before hurrying off in pursuit of Nicholas.

Suddenly, it was as if all the fun and expectation had been sucked out of the evening. I did my best to smile back at her, to hide the surge of jealousy and disappointment that swept through me. Thandiwe could not possibly have known the hurtful effect that her words would have. She had seen my wedding ring. I had told her about my husband. She had obviously assumed, given what I had told her, that I was a happily married woman who couldn't wait to get out of here and back home.

And I had been, only seventy-two hours ago. Where had it all gone wrong?

On feet that were suddenly leaden, I trailed toward the party area, to find Miriam standing next to Mrs. Groenewald, a well-groomed matriarch who was now in conversation with Nicholas.

"Lovely to see you, Mr. de Lanoy," the matriarch said. "Hasn't this bridge been an inconvenience? Poor Colette, my niece, was supposed to attend her honors degree celebration at Wits yesterday and she has not been able to get out of here. It is so disappointing for her. Colette, do come here and meet Mr. de Lanoy."

A slender young woman with sparkling green eyes and thick, wavy auburn hair stepped forward and shook Nicholas's hand. She was taller than me—in her high heels she stood nearly eye to eye with him.

Nicholas glanced over his right shoulder and I thought he might be checking to see where I was. Well, I didn't want to rain on their parade. I ducked to the left, rounded a pillar, and found myself standing in a paved barbecue area where a fire was blazing. A rotund grey-haired man in a white short-sleeved collared shirt was poking at the coals with a stick. We made our introductions—he was Kobus Bosnik from the farm on the other side of the hill.

"Would you like a drink?" he asked me.

"I'd love some white wine." I wasn't in a champagne mood any more. While Kobus was organizing me a glass, I peeked round the pillar again to see, with a bitter stab of jealousy, that Nicholas had his back to me and had been drawn into a tight little group on the far side of the room with Mrs. Groenewald on his left and Colette on his right.

While I watched, Colette laughed at something Nicholas had said to her, her full, red-lipsticked mouth parting. She placed her left hand on his shoulder and he leaned toward her. I turned away, unable to watch any more, grateful when a minute later, Kobus brought me a brimming glass of white wine.

"My wife's stuck in town," he told me. "She's been there for three days now—couldn't get back because of the flood. I've been living on TV dinners cooked outside on the barbecue. After the first time, I realized you need to take them out of the plastic container before you heat them up on the coals. And, worst of all, my wife took my credit card with her when she left. She's been phoning me to say that every place in town is booked up apart from the brand new five-star *Hyatt*. No other accommodation to be had, apparently. So that's where she's staying, and I'm paying!"

He roared with laughter and I joined in. Mr. Bosnik was a natural comedian. Half an hour later we were the center of a group including Miriam and Joshua, and a couple of other locals. He had a fresh beer in his hand and I was halfway through my second glass of wine.

"So we've driven this road for twenty years now," he said, "and I swear, until this time last week, I'd never seen the pothole just before the intersection that was so deep we actually expected somebody to come along and ask about mining rights. I mean, you've never seen anything like it. My tire was shredded. Shredded. So there I am, with no truck, and a whole load of macadamias in the back, to deliver to the *Spar* by that afternoon, except by then I thought I was the one who was nuts."

"You are nuts," one of the other men commented, to general laughter.

"So then I start looking for my car jack. You know, to change the tire. And I didn't have one in the vehicle, so I walk all the way down to the main road, and along comes a minibus full of tourists. So I step into the middle of the road and flag it down. My luck, the damn driver is half German and mostly deaf. He leans out of the window and asks if he can help. So I say, 'Car jack. I need a car jack.'"

"And then?"

"And then he sticks his head back in again and they close all the windows. I start phoning my wife to ask her for a set of tools, but a minute later I hear sirens over the hill, coming my way, and there's a helicopter circling overhead. And the flippin' cops from over in Nelspruit pitch up with the chopper and three emergency vehicles—oh, and an ambulance, because the German bus driver thought I'd been car-jacked. Because I'd said to him, 'car jack.' And by the time the story got through to the police, they thought the whole tour bus had been car-jacked!"

Amid the laughter that followed, Joshua leaned over to me and asked in a low voice, "Where is Mr. Nicholas?"

I shrugged, then gestured in the direction of the entertainment area. "Last seen in there, being introduced to a young redhead and clearly getting along very well with her."

Joshua had seen Nicholas and me in the swimming pool together—he knew how things were between us. Now he stared at me, frowning in concern, clearly not knowing what an appropriate response to this might be.

Nor did I. I sipped my wine and tried not to think about how angry I felt and how confused I was. Tried instead to laugh at my entertaining companions, and not to imagine Nicholas in the room next door, turning all his charm on to the gorgeous Colette. I stood in miserable silence while Joshua offered me silent sympathy and Miriam, poised and smiling, squeezed my arm briefly.

CHAPTER 14

MY SECOND GLASS OF wine was almost finished when two warm, strong hands clasped me around my waist. My heart accelerated instantly. Mr. Bosnik paused mid-sentence in yet another of his funny stories.

"Well, hello, Nick!" he said. "Where've you been?"

"Doing the rounds inside," he said. "I've come to say hello, and check up on how my guest is faring." I arched away from his touch but his grasp followed me, warm and sure. "Good to see you, Kobus. Mrs. B. not home yet?"

"No. I've been making emergency arrangements with the bank. I should get the card paid off in another fifty years or so."

Nicholas laughed. "Is everyone okay for a drink?" he asked. "My glass needs a refill. So does yours," he said, removing mine from my grasp.

"No, I'm fine, honestly," I told him, but he took my hand and led me away from the laughing group and back into the entertainment area, where rock music was pulsing from the speakers and, I could see, the two Groenewald women were craning their necks to keep track of him.

I tugged my hand out of his.

"Really, I'm good," I told him, shouting to be heard over the beat. "I'm having a lovely time. You must… Go on, enjoy yourself." I gestured to the group he'd recently left—discreetly, I hoped.

"Glad *you're* having a lovely time. I'd be having more fun with you." He removed the champagne bottle from the large ice-filled tub where it had been chilling. "Come on. Let's go somewhere quieter."

My ears were ringing from the music as we walked out of the entertainment area and through the treed garden into the darkening evening.

"I saw they built a bonfire on the other side of the garden," Nicholas said, and ahead I could see the flicker of flames in the center of a large sandy clearing.

He sat on a wooden bench on the far side of the bonfire and patted the seat beside him.

"Sit."

The hiss of the champagne cork sounded very loud in the silence. I sat next to him. Our knees brushed, then pressed together.

"We only have one glass," I said.

"We'll share." He filled it slowly and carefully before handing it to me. The bubbles sparkled on the surface, bursting on my lips as I sipped.

"I feel bad for leaving you alone," he said. "I'm sorry."

"You didn't leave me. I left you. I saw you were otherwise occupied. I didn't want to interfere."

"Otherwise monopolized," he said with a rueful smile.

"She looks like a lovely girl."

"I'm sure she is."

"Isn't she your type?"

"Erin, I don't have a type."

"Well, 'scuse me for assuming that a sexy young redhead might be your type," I said, letting my voice drip with sarcasm. "Or do you prefer blondes?"

I knew that if I'd spoken like that to Vince it would have enraged him. But Nicholas only smiled. "How much wine have you had?" he asked, sounding amused.

"Only two glasses. Poured for me by your friendly neighbor Kobus."

"Ah. So more like four glasses, then, if he was pouring."

"Do I appear drunk?"

"No. You appear honest and outspoken. I'm liking it."

He passed me the champagne and I took a large gulp.

"Go back to your redhead," I told him. "She's beautiful."

"She's not my redhead."

"She could be. She wants to be."

"And I don't."

"What does she have an honors degree in?"

"Um. She did tell me… or her aunt did. Er… fine arts, I think. Art of some kind, definitely."

"Oh, great," I said, hating her all the more.

"Why do you say that?"

"Because art's what I wanted to study. I would have studied it if I hadn't fucked up my life beforehand."

"Tell me why that happened." He put his arm round me and I leaned against him.

"No. I'm not going to tell you."

"And I'm not going to stop asking."

I watched him pour more champagne, while my resentful thoughts toward Colette bubbled.

"I can see your future mapped out now, Nicholas," I told him. "In a few years you'll be married. Probably, you'll have had a big wedding ceremony at the lodge. You'll have a couple of beautiful kids running around. Maybe you'll be faithful to your wife. Maybe you won't. But that's your life. That's the way it will go. I can predict it. And I'm sure you'll be very complacent with your happy ending."

He was silent for a moment while the crackle of the flaming logs snapped in my ears.

Then he let out a sigh.

"If only happy endings were so easy," he said. "You know, that's what I was thinking earlier on, when I was standing with the Groenewalds. That is exactly what was going through my mind. Here I am, being set up with a very suitable, attractive, single young woman, and everybody's hope and expectation would be that, best case, in a few years we'd be where you've just described. Even I tried to go along with it—for the first thirty seconds, anyway."

"Well, I agree life is not always simple," I said.

"For a number of important reasons, Erin, my life is not going to go that route." He sipped from the glass, then handed it to me.

"What are those reasons?"

"There are some I won't tell you."

"I'll keep asking."

"Okay, then. I'll tell you one. You're a reason," he said, and his words surprised me so much I almost fell off the bench and onto the carefully raked, pale sand below.

"Me?"

"Yes."

"You mean—you don't want to fool around with anybody else while I'm still here?" I was clutching at possible explanations, not understanding him at all.

"Well, that's true, actually. I'm a faithful type, in my own way. I only commit adultery with one married woman at a time," he said, offering a mischievous grin. "But it's not that. It's… hell, I don't know. All I know is I can't stop thinking about you. When I was standing with the Groenewalds, I didn't want to be with them. I wanted to be with you, Erin."

Suddenly I felt as if I could not breathe.

He put the bottle and the glass carefully down on the sandy ground.

My head was whirling now, partly from a fair amount of alcohol on an empty stomach, and partly from his words, his closeness. Nicholas must never know that I felt the same way about him, too, I told myself. I should not even take what he'd said too seriously. Clearly, he had a marvelous line in smooth talk, which I was sure he gave all the girls. Coming from me, though, those same words would show vulnerability.

Then I forgot my stern self-talk as he leaned close to me and with eagerness I met his kiss. The touch of his lips had the same instant effect on me as it had done before, melting my insides, making me lustful, needy, reckless. His hands smoothed up my legs, pushing the silken skirt of my dress higher, catching his breath as his fingers traveled all the way up my thighs to encounter only bare and naked skin.

"No panties… you have no idea what a turn-on that is," he murmured. "What it does to me."

"That isn't exactly by choice. I only have one pair with me. I can't wear them all the time," I protested. My voice was complaining—rather breathlessly, I had to admit—but my body was not. I could not contain my desire for him. I was pushing my hips toward him, silently begging for him to touch me more intimately, to fulfill my limitless craving for him.

"You are so sexy. With or without underwear." He stroked his fingertips lightly over my cleft, and I caught my breath at the sensuality of that gossamer touch. "It's just that without… you offer me far too much temptation. You can't imagine how badly I've been needing you. And I can't sit here knowing that you are here… uncovered, open, waiting… not without doing something about it."

The movements of his hand and my body had caused my dress to ruche up around my thighs, and now he encouraged me to lean back before lifting the front of the skirt higher and bending to kiss the soft, sensitive skin of my inner thigh.

"Nicholas!" I whispered. "I… ooh… you can't do this now. What if somebody sees us?"

"We're on the far side of the fire, and it's very dark out. If anyone walks this way we'll hear them on the gravel path. Then we'll have time to make a plan."

His breath was warm on my skin. He trailed kisses up my thigh before parting my lips gently with his fingers and sliding his tongue in between. Desire bloomed inside me; the orgasm I'd had earlier that day only serving to make me hungrier for his touch now.

With exquisite tenderness, his tongue stroked over my clitoris, the soft thrill of the touch causing me to gasp. I realized that my body was yielding to him, any resistance I might have mustered ebbing away before I could even consider it. I could not have moved if I had wanted to. All I could think about, all that mattered, were his intimate caresses. His tongue slid warmly over my delicate flesh, he sucked my lips in ways that made me bite back a moan of delight.

Such wicked intimacy, and in a place where we could so easily be interrupted. Would I have time to warn him—would I have any wits left to pull myself together if somebody did appear? Oh, this was bold and entirely wrong—but so addictively exciting. I was loving this; loving how much he turned me on, and that he seemed to find me as impossible to resist as I found him.

The thrill of what we were doing was only intensifying the sensory rapture he was offering me.

He circled the tip of his tongue lightly over my clitoris until I was gasping with delight, then thrust his tongue deep inside me, and I felt my fingernails scrape over the wooden corner of the bench as my grip tightened. Sensing my movement, he found my hand with his own and grasped it, his fingers twined in mine and his thumb caressing my palm.

I was throbbing, opened to him, he already had me trembling on the edge. He circled my clitoris again, fluttering his tongue over the swollen nubbin of bliss, then slid a finger inside me. I gasped with delight as he began slowly, gently fucking me with two fingers. With each thrust, his fingertips massaged my G-spot. I could feel myself starting to tighten inside as heat suffused my lower body. I knew that he was going to make me orgasm again soon… easily, effortlessly.

And then, over the thrumming of the blood in my own ears, I heard another and far less welcome sound—the noise of low voices and footsteps scrunching over the gravel path behind me.

I froze into place, listening. I found myself suddenly, intensely aware of every movement that Nicholas was making. The sensual, sliding exploration of his fingers; the soft flickering of his tongue.

"… yes, I've got a dish for the meat." It was Thandiwe's voice.

"Have you seen Nicholas?" Berndt spoke, and his words sent a thrill of apprehension through me. "Mrs. Groenewald was looking for him."

"I haven't seen him for a little while."

"Who's that over there by the fire?"

For a moment, I wished I could feign deafness, or preferably disappear into the ground. Then, taking a deep breath, I looked over my shoulder and called, "It's me, Erin."

"Ah, Erin. You're doing okay there on your own?"

At the words, Nicholas's fingers slid more deeply inside me and I caught my breath. With him sprawled in front of me on the log bench, there was no way Thandiwe or Berndt, who were standing behind me, could see him. Not in this flickering darkness... not unless they came closer, or I gave the game away.

"I'm doing fine, thanks. Star gazing." I fought for control, to keep my voice steady.

"Dinner's ready in about ten minutes. You must come and eat."

"Oh, I will," I called back.

"Do you know where Nicholas is?" Berndt's voice this time.

He's right here on this bench, giving me the most divine oral sex I've ever had...

"Last I saw, he was inside, talking to the Groenewalds," I said, deciding to exact some sweet revenge. "He seemed to be getting along very well with Colette."

Bad idea to rile him on this subject, Erin, I realized immediately. Bad, bad idea.

Nicholas's other hand pushed further underneath me and with a start I felt his finger, slick and wet, stroking gently over my anus.

No *way*. This was too outrageous... far too forbidden. I'd managed to remain coherent so far, but I knew I could not possibly conduct a conversation while he was stimulating me in that way. And nor could I yell "Stop!" Discreetly, I tried to shove his head away with the palm of my hand, but it was like trying to move the Rock of Gibraltar.

"Oh, I'm so glad to hear that. She is a lovely young woman," Berndt said.

"I think they seem... very well suited," I responded. My voice sounded wobbly, my heart was pounding, but I might as well keep agreeing with him now because I was sure nothing I said now would distract my lover from his mission of wickedness.

Slowly, sensually, taking his time over the actions, Nicholas slid the tip of his finger into my backside. I had to bite my lip to keep from moaning at the audacious pleasure of it.

"Can I bring you another drink?" Berndt called.

Oh, God, now Nicholas was pumping his finger gently in and out of my rear, each time pushing in a little deeper. It felt amazingly, shamefully good. He nibbled my clitoris, pressed into my G-spot with the fingers of his other hand, and I felt an urgent heat flood my body.

"Join you… in a minute," I said, then clamped my lips together hard to stifle a cry of delight. His fingers were all the way inside me, his tongue teasing pulses of ecstasy from my throbbing clit. I was filled by him; opened and utterly possessed, and then, thank God, the scrunching of feet on gravel indicated my hosts were making their way to the entertainment area.

I let out a deep, fast breath as I came painfully hard, thrusting myself against him. I twined my fingers through his hair and tugged his head closer as pleasure spiked through me again and again.

He slipped his fingers out of me. Extricating himself from under my skirt, he sat up, locked his arms around me and kissed me deeply. I tasted myself in his mouth, the flavor of my own arousal on his lips. I kissed him back hard, realizing that while this orgasm had sated my hunger for him, it had also made me greedy for more.

In the firelight I could see his face, taut with lust.

Reaching down for the glass, he gulped a mouthful of champagne and kissed me, letting some of the cold, bubbly liquid froth into my mouth. The sensation was incredible. It made me feel dizzy, as if I were floating.

"Do we dare?" he whispered, and I only realized what he meant when he unbuttoned and unzipped his jeans and, with practiced expertise, took a condom out of his pocket and rolled it on to sheathe his engorged cock.

"Not now," I breathed, suppressing an amazed giggle. This man was bad, and I was loving it far too much.

"Nicholas, they're going to come looking for me in a few minutes…" I was breathing hard, and although the risk of being interrupted was adding to my thrill, what was really turning me on was the thought of having him inside me again. I was throbbing, needy, desperate to feel that thick, hard manhood that was his essence.

"Oh, I think we can risk it, Erin." The firelight illuminated the devilish glint in his eye. He shifted sideways so that he was straddling the narrow wooden seat of the bench. "Come sit on my lap." His strong arms lifted me into place and I locked my arms around his neck, my face pressed against his, feeling the light rasp of his stubble against my cheek. Oh, God, I could feel him, his wide, swollen head thrusting between my slick, wet lips. I gave a tiny moan of pleasure as he entered me and he shifted his hips in response to it, breathing hard, clamping me down onto him as he arched himself deep inside me.

"If anyone sees us now they might just think we're having a conversation," he whispered, and in his voice I could hear the same wickedness I'd seen in his eyes. He was breathing hard, his chest rising and falling against my own, and the musky scent of his skin filled my nostrils. Holding me tight, he eased himself almost all the way out of me before pushing slowly in again and again. I sank onto him, loving the deep fullness of the sensation, loving that even while I was on top of him, he was in total, masterful control.

"A very close, very intimate one."

Now he was circling his hips, moving his cock inside me, stretching me deliciously. I dug my fingers into his back, the deep throbbing in the pit of my stomach growing almost painfully intense.

"Don't tell me you're starting to enjoy this," he whispered a while later. "I thought you were going to ask me to stop."

"Don't… stop…." How on earth was he managing to hold a conversation, albeit rather breathlessly, when I was now barely capable of getting a word out?

"Do you like to fuck when there's a risk of being caught?" he murmured, and his words caused me to writhe in guilty delight, another orgasm brewing inside me like a summer storm.

"Yes," I breathed.

His teeth nibbled at my ear, then bit the lobe just hard enough that I jumped, the involuntary movement causing him to buck his hips and gasp.

"You… are so fucking sexy." He licked my earlobe, then flicked his tongue in and out of my ear, the warm, wet caress so pleasurable it was sending my senses into overload. I was helpless, almost sobbing with arousal, every nerve ending in my body clamoring for more.

I knew we had to be quiet, but it felt to me as if the entire world was holding its breath. I was shaking with tension at the thrilling, shameful risk of discovery. I didn't know if it would be possible not to cry out. And then Nicholas pushed inside me again, the movement small but deep, but it was enough to trigger my orgasm. Somehow managing to swallow a moan, I buried my face in his neck, tasting his skin, abandoning my control as I spasmed around him tight and hard.

A moment later, betrayed only by the shuddering of his hips and crushing firmness of his arms around me, Nicholas came. His body barely moved as he experienced an orgasm so brutally powerful that I felt every pulsing jerk of his cock inside me.

"I don't know how much more of this I can take," I whispered to him, when I could speak again. "This is too intense. One way or another, my heart may give out soon."

His breathless laugh tickled my hair. "I know. I feel the same."

As we disengaged and did our best to straighten our clothing, the rumble of thunder and a flash of lightning from the horizon reminded me that it was far from certain that the bridge would be getting fixed the next day. Another of those storms could easily see the river flood again.

My legs felt unsteady from too much alcohol and too much sex. I was ravenously hungry and the aroma of well-cooked meat was drawing me in like a vulture to a kill. When we walked inside, everyone was already eating and we were the object of some curious glances. Mrs. Groenewald had saved just one place at the table where she and her niece were seated, but Nicholas politely refused it, and after piling our plates with food, we sat on our own together at the bar.

I carefully avoided Thandiwe's gaze, but when I took our empty plates through to the kitchen, I walked in at the same time she was walking out. She looked at me closely and I could only guess what she saw. My hair mussed, my dress creased, my lips swollen and my skin still flushed and sensitive from the friction of Nicholas's stubble.

She met my gaze as we stacked the plates, and in her eyes I saw a blend of confusion and concern.

Thandiwe had seen us walk in together, late for supper, after I had told her I thought Nicholas was with the Groenewalds. From her face, I guessed she had put two and two together. I felt that some kind of explanation or apology was in order and, clearly, so did she.

"I'm sorry," I said, feeling ashamed. What must she think of me?

"I—when I said what I did earlier, about Colette—I'm sorry, Erin. That was insensitive of me. I didn't know you and Nicholas were…"

I tried for a worldly smile, but it didn't really work and in the end I just stared back at her with what I supposed was much the same expression as her own.

"I didn't really know either, till a little while ago."

"Just be careful, my dear," she said, squeezed my hand, and walked out of the kitchen, leaving me to wonder what exactly she had meant by the words.

CHAPTER 15

I DON'T REMEMBER MUCH more about the evening. We had another glass of champagne, and after our dinner, rejoined the group to sit at Kobus's table where I laughed my head off at his series of jokes, and so did Nicholas. Discreetly, under the table, we held hands, Nicholas's fingers caressing my palm. I remember at one stage exchanging a glance with Joshua across the table and, if I recall correctly, we gave each other a relieved smile.

It was well after midnight when we left, with Nicholas driving slowly and following Joshua's taillights up the hill. I was trying to conduct a one-woman sing-along, the theme being *Phantom of the Opera*. My singing voice is not my strongest attribute but, after a few drinks, I love to exercise it. When he wasn't singing along with me, Nicholas was laughing so hard he was nearly driving off the road. All I could think about was what fun we were having. It seemed like a very long time since I'd enjoyed myself so much.

We then had a discussion about bedrooms. I insisted I was going back to my room. He overrode my decision, giving a reason that seemed compelling at the time but which subsequently escaped my memory.

I told him I needed to brush my teeth and he told me to go and brush my teeth, but to come back afterwards, or he was going to come and find me.

I made my way back to my room. I brushed my teeth and washed my face. It was strange to come back from an evening out and have no make-up to remove. It occurred to me that Nicholas had never seen me with make-up, apart from what I'd been wearing on the day the car went into the river, which by the time he had rescued me, had certainly been a smeared mess. He'd never smelt me wearing my own perfume, only the lightly scented cosmetics in my bedroom.

He had only ever seen me as I was.

Vince, on the other hand, had seldom seen me without make-up and when I didn't wear it, he urged me to do so.

I pondered this fact fuzzily for a while, but without reaching any significant conclusion. Then I turned on my phone, glad that thanks to all the alcohol, I did not feel the usual surge of dread as I waited to see what communications I had received.

There had been seven more missed calls from Vince, and despite my state of drunken relaxation, I felt my stomach twist with anxiety.

The phone beeped. Finally, at a quarter past eight that evening, he had left a message.

His tone was terse and hard.

"I don't care what time it is when you get this. Call me."

Before I had time to get too worked up about speaking to him, I phoned him back.

He answered within one ring. "Jesus Christ, Erin, for fuck's sake, where have you been?"

"Nice to speak to you, too, Vince," I retorted, noticing I was slurring the words.

"This is not a fucking joke. I have been trying to get hold of you all day. Where the fuck have you been?"

"This morning I was helping to fix a broken fence, to guard against poachers and cheetahs," I stifled a hiccough. "And this evening, the neighbors hosted a dinner for everyone on this side of the river, and I've been over at their farm."

"And you didn't fucking call me back?"

"I did. I left a message for you. If it was so urgent, why didn't you leave any messages for me? I did check my voicemail at lunchtime."

"Because I assume that when I try to get hold of my own fucking wife, I don't need to leave messages. And that when you see it's me calling you would treat it as urgent. Why didn't you keep your phone on you, for fuck's sake?"

"Don't speak to me that way, Vince."

"I'll speak to you how I fucking want. You're drunk, aren't you?"

Rage simmered inside me and my finger hovered over the disconnect button. Then I decided to give him the benefit of the doubt.

"I had a couple of drinks with dinner. Big deal. And I didn't take my phone with me. I had no purse, no pockets, and nowhere to put the damned phone. So I left it here."

"Christ, you can be stupid sometimes!"

"Vince!"

"I had a helicopter organized!" he screamed at me, and I felt myself go cold inside.

"Why didn't you tell me earlier?"

"I was waiting for you to call me back so that I could arrange a pickup with the pilot. One of Helena's friends was spending some time in the Kruger and said he'd be able to fly by your place and get you out. As a favor. So we spent the whole morning waiting for you to call back. Then he delayed his flight again and we waited the whole afternoon. And meanwhile you were doing other things. You didn't bother to call back. You were just doing whatever you felt like doing, because it's all about you, isn't it, Erin? Really, it always has been, you stupid, fucking, self-centered…"

Abruptly, I jammed my finger onto the disconnect button. I couldn't bear to hear any more of this. With hands trembling from haste, because I wanted to get it done before he could call me back, I turned the phone off again.

I felt far more sober than I had ten minutes ago. The fuzziness, the laughter, the sense of fun had all evaporated. I felt small, crushed, and very alone.

I was going to break my promise to go back to Nicholas's bedroom, but it seemed like a small thing compared to the much bigger and more important vows I'd already smashed. I locked my door, drank two glasses of water, collapsed onto my bed, and pulled the sheets over me. Outside, I heard the crashing of thunder. I thought I'd be kept awake, either by the storm or by the tumult of my own thoughts, but within a few minutes I was deeply asleep.

❄ ❄ ❄

I was awakened by another clap of thunder and the violent hammering of rain.

Opening my eyes, I found the grey daylight unbearably bright. My mouth was a desert and my tongue felt like sandpaper.

Coffee. I needed coffee. And chocolate fudge brownies—my hangover cure of choice. Since I guessed chocolate brownies would be in short supply in the lodge, I decided to settle for a serious dose of caffeine. I fixed myself some in the kitchen, together with a slice of toast. It was six-thirty in the morning, too early for anybody else to be around. I wondered briefly if Nicholas was still asleep. However, when I walked back to my room with my breakfast, I heard the rhythmic slapping and thudding of the punching bag. He was in the gym, sweating out his hangover—and his anger, I supposed.

I stopped by the library, which was lined with mahogany shelves containing the most eclectic collection of books I'd ever seen. Many of them were medical books on everything from basic biology to the etymology of obscure diseases, but they stood spine to spine with works of fiction both old and new: travel writing, history books, biographies, and a whole shelf on art. The shelves were not all systematically arranged. *Lung Disease in the Tropics* was slotted between *Autobiography of a Yogi* and *Jefferson's Letters*, while in the middle of a shelf of the classics, I found the *Kama Sutra* as well as the *Story of O*. I smiled when I saw he had three copies of *Life of Pi*. Perhaps that was one of his favorites, just as it was one of mine.

In the end, though, all I chose was a colorfully illustrated South African recipe book. If you can't eat sweet baked goods, you can at least read about them, I thought. This would be the literary equivalent of comfort food—a pleasant distraction from the physical pain of my hangover and the more hurtful emotional pain I felt when I thought about Vince's words.

Sam had emailed back and I opened her response eagerly, looking forward to getting her opinion on the situation.

Girlfriend!! she wrote. *Holy cow. I had no idea that all of this was going on. This is very, very, VERY complicated. Sheesh… you've been unfaithful to Vince? Wow. That is not what I ever thought would happen. You're probably thinking I'm gonna say you're wrong to have done it, and you should go for counseling. That if you're going through a rough patch with Vince, you need to try and fix it. But actually, I feel the opposite way.*

I think maybe this fling was a good thing for you. You might hate me for saying this but I have to be truthful. I think Vince is a prick. I can't stand how he treats you, and his behavior is alienating you from your friends. I promised myself I would never tell you this, but at your engagement party, I ended up alone with him in the bar for awhile, and, do you know, he was trying to come on to me?

Anyway, this is probably too much info, and I apologize, because if you stay with him, our friendship is probably over now, but the thing is that if you stay with him, I'm never gonna see you anyway, so there's no harm in being truthful, right? I just wish you all the best, and if you do leave him, I'm always here for you… you can call anytime, or come and stay for as long as you need to. Love you, and take care.

I closed the email quickly, not wanting to take in what it said. Then I opened it and read it again.

Sam thought Vince had come onto her?

Surely not. She must have been wrong about that. Perhaps she was exaggerating what had happened, or she remembered it wrong. Vince would never have done such a thing at our engagement party, with one of my best friends… would he?

I stared out of the window at the grey sheets of rain lashing the glass. Thunder cracked again, directly overhead, and the sound of the rain was replaced briefly by the rattling of hail. The elements were conspiring against me for sure. No work would be done on the bridge with this storm raging, and if I were especially unlucky, the sandbags shoring up the bank would be washed away.

Great.

I couldn't let myself think about the conversation I'd had with Vince last night. How demeaning it had felt to be sworn at that way. Was Sam's observation correct? Did people really think my husband treated me badly? I knew Vince had been angry—but why did he have to vent his temper that way? Maybe I should buy him a big red punching bag.

And, once again, I felt unfairly manipulated. If he'd only left a message earlier, or even texted me, I would have known how urgent it was and would have called him back.

Worse still, he'd been in touch with Helena. In spite of the fact that he'd obviously done so with a view of helping me, his words were troubling. He'd said "we spent the whole morning waiting for you to call back." Had Vince meant he and the pilot? He and Helena? Did that mean Helena had, in fact, flown up to see him? And even if I hadn't answered his call, why hadn't he just told the helicopter pilot to fly to Leopard Rock regardless? He knew I would have been there... it wasn't like there was anywhere else for me to go.

His words had not only wounded me, they had crushed me. He had the ability to make me feel as if I deserved his insults, and now this was causing me to become angry and resentful.

It was strange the effect that distance had. When we'd been living together, after similar fights, I had done everything I could to placate him and to restore the peace, and it had taken a day at most for things to get back to normal.

Now, without the constant demands of his presence, there was time for me to see the situation in a new perspective—to gain some distance from the effect that his moods and his criticisms invariably had on me. The problem was that I did not want the distance. It felt unsafe to have to think about Vince in this way. I longed suddenly to be back together with him. When we were together, the fights had not seemed to matter. I'd never felt anger or resentment. Vicious as they were, when we were in proximity to each other, it had been a whole lot easier to make up.

I wished I could go back to feeling the way I had done in the past. That I was incredibly lucky to have married this man—this renowned photographer, who had received international acclaim for his work, who had become wealthy through his own perseverance and talent, and who, of all the women in the world he could have chosen, had married me.

I turned on my phone, intending to phone Vince and apologize for hanging up on him, but when I called him, it rang and rang before going through to voicemail.

With a sinking heart I realized he was still angry with me.

I read Sam's email once more and then deleted it. She had been right when she'd said it was too much info. Her words, in harsh black and white, were so troubling to me that I was not able to respond to them—not even with a thank you.

By the time I'd filled in the insurance form and made some phone calls to find out more about the car's condition, the rain had eased up. In my stash of clothing, I found a large waterproof jacket with a hood. It would do for now. I was going to walk down to the river and see exactly what the situation was with the bridge—and, this time, I was going to take my phone with me and keep it turned on.

Putting it carefully in the Velcro pocket of the jacket, I set off.

I'd thought the distance to be a couple of miles, but even though it was mostly downhill, it was also somewhat longer. It took me more than an hour of plowing through muddy sandbanks and splashing across puddles. By the time I reached it, I was limping on at least one blister from my ill-fitting shoes, and the sight that greeted me was not what I had hoped for.

The water had torn a gaping hole in the carefully sandbagged bank. The river was in full flood again, the waters murky and grey, fast-moving and dangerous looking. There was not a soul in sight, although a tarpaulin nearby, weighed down with rocks, presumably covered some of the tools and equipment that would be used when, and if, the damned river ever stopped overflowing its banks.

The only ray of hope was that two long steel girders had been placed over the sandbags, stretching all the way across the river to the other side. They were still in position. So hopefully, if the sandbags could be shored up again, building might be able to start tomorrow. It didn't have to be a proper road. Even a small walkway would do for me, for now.

The swishing of tires behind me made me look round, and with a sinking of my heart I saw Nicholas at the wheel of his Land Cruiser.

He climbed out and gave me the barest nod of greeting. His face looked as hard as I'd ever seen it, and I wondered what had happened to make him angry.

Could it have been because I broke my promise to him by not coming back to his bedroom last night?

Well, if it was—if he was petty enough to get in a mood over that—let him stew in his own ill-temper, I thought, with a flash of defiance. I had my own bigger problems to deal with, far more important and far-reaching than the sulkiness of a womanizer who for once had not gotten his way.

I turned my back to him and stared out at the rushing water. At least the walk and the fresh air had cleared my head and banished the hangover.

"They're not going to be able to fix the bridge until a dam wall further upriver has been repaired," Nicholas said behind me. "It burst in the first rains, which is why it keeps flooding now. They're going to be working on the wall later, weather permitting."

I didn't turn around and nor did I acknowledge him.

Then, from my pocket, I heard the ringing of my phone.

Hastily, I splashed my way through a large puddle, heading further down the hill away from him. The sound of the water was very loud here. Vince was calling, and it was time to mend my bridges… figuratively, at least.

"Vince, honey," I said. "Hi. I'm sorry about last night. How're you doing?"

"Not good." His voice was tight and sharp.

"I'm really sorry for hanging up on you," I said. "And it was thoughtless of me not to take the phone with me yesterday. I should have known it was important. I'm so sorry."

"Where are you?" he asked. "Are you in the shower?"

"I'm down here at the river. Some of the sandbags they put in yesterday have been washed away. It's going to take another two or three days to get this bridge repaired, but as soon as they do, I'm coming over it." I laughed, even though it felt forced. "I'm going to walk over on foot, if necessary, to be with you again."

"It's too late for that," he said, and the words as well as his tone made my stomach clench.

"How do you mean?"

"Erin, I can't deal with this anymore. You are not the girl I married. What has happened to you? You used to be so devoted. You were so caring. And now, you've changed. Or rather, I don't know if you've changed, or whether this is the real you and everything I knew before has been a lie."

"Vince!" Aware that Nicholas was still behind me, I hastily lowered my voice again. "I've always been the same person. I've just been under a lot of stress the past few days, and I know you have, too."

"No." His voice was cold. "It started before that. You've been showing me your real side for a while now. Flirting with other men deliberately. You wouldn't have been washed away in that car if you'd chosen to drive with me."

"Vince, are you insane?" Again, I was aware I'd raised my voice, and had to struggle to control myself. "You told me to get into the other car. You said you didn't want to drive with me."

"You're right. I didn't. But what I find strange is that you didn't fight for it. You agreed immediately. It was almost as if you wanted to go into that other car, to be alone with that young driver. I saw the way he was looking at you. How do I know you haven't been with him this whole time?"

"Bulewi's not even here! He managed to escape to the other side of the river. And you're not to talk badly of him after he tried to save me. If he hadn't undone my seatbelt, I would have died."

I'd hoped my honesty would shame Vince into silence, but it was as if he hadn't even listened to my outburst.

"If you loved me, you would have insisted on coming with me. It was a test, Erin, and you failed it."

"But…"

"And why did you end up lagging so far behind me? Was that also deliberate?"

"No! It was not. The storm was terrible, and you were driving like a…"

"I think we need a trial separation, Erin."

"No," I said again, whispering out the words through cold lips.

"I'm booked to fly back to New York on Friday and I'm taking that flight. I'm not waiting around here for days or weeks for some mythical bridge to be repaired."

"It was not a mythical bridge!" I insisted. "It was a real one, and I'm standing where it was right now. You didn't even bother to come here to see. I would have thought you'd have been camped out in a tent on the other side, waiting for me to be able to cross over. Instead, you're holed up in five-star comfort."

"Shut up! You've milked this situation already for all it's worth," he yelled angrily. "If you were really stuck, you would have phoned me back yesterday so I could come and get you. If you don't fly back with me, I'm going to pack up your belongings so that when you do choose to come back to the States, you can move out and look for somewhere else to stay."

"Vince, no!" I could hear the panic in my voice.

"This is your decision. Not mine. You're the one who made this all go wrong."

"If I could swim across this damned river right now, I would!"

"You had the chance to come back to me yesterday," he said heavily. "You didn't take it."

"Look, why don't you charter a helicopter from your side and come get me?"

"Like I said, I'm flying back when we're booked to leave. And now, I have work to do. I had to cancel shooting yesterday, so I'm going into the bush now. My guide's waiting outside. Don't try to contact me today because I won't be available."

He disconnected without saying another word.

CHAPTER 16

"Shit!" I said loudly.

I turned off my phone to conserve what remaining battery I had, moved away from the river and, without acknowledging Nicholas, headed up the steep bank and marched past the place where his car was parked.

"What's the matter?" he asked.

I didn't answer, just kept walking, but a minute later, the throbbing of the truck's engine behind me told me that my intent to stomp off back to the lodge alone was going to be thwarted.

"Get in," he called through the open window.

"No, thanks."

"Erin, get in. You've walked the whole way down here in the wet in those ill-fitting shoes, and if you haven't blisters already, you soon shall." He leaned over, opened the door. "Come on."

I trudged over to the car, climbed in, slammed the door.

"Trouble in paradise?" he asked.

I turned on him furiously. "At this moment, I do not need your comments, which in any case are not funny. My husband has just told me that he thinks we need a trial separation." I was crying now, my shoulders shaking, tears flooding my eyes.

Nicholas stopped the car in the shade by the muddy roadside, and cut the engine. He waited for a minute until I'd regained some control over my emotions, before asking, "Why does he want that?"

"He had a helicopter ready to bring me out yesterday." My face was burning with shame. "The pilot was waiting to fly here. But because I didn't have my phone with me, he couldn't."

Blinking tears away, I saw Nicholas regarding me, his face still hard.

"Why the trial separation? I'm confused, Erin. You didn't have your phone with you. So what? Did you know he was going to try and get a helicopter to you?"

I sniffed. "I had no idea."

"So you had no idea your husband was trying to organize you a helicopter. But the pilot could have flown here regardless. Everyone in the area knows the coordinates for Leopard Rock."

I shrugged.

"So because you didn't have your phone with you when he suddenly decided to try and rescue you, and he didn't tell the pilot to come here anyway, he now thinks you should have a trial separation?"

I gave a shaky laugh. When Nicholas put it that way it did, of course, sound stupid.

"It's not just that," I told him.

"Well, what else has changed? What's gone so suddenly wrong between yesterday and today?"

Another question I couldn't answer.

"You don't understand the situation," I said.

"Well, clearly I don't. But if that's all that has happened then there's no cause to be so upset." He drew in a breath as if he was going to say something else to me, but then shook his head. Instead, he started the car and headed up the road.

"What?" I asked.

"Nothing."

"You were going to say something."

"I was going to tell you why I was so angry earlier. But now I'm not."

"Why not?"

"Because I don't think that what I was going to say will make a difference to what you have decided to believe."

"Oh." I considered his words for a short while. Did his anger have something to do with Vince? It certainly sounded like it.

Nicholas drew a deep breath. "You want me to be honest?"

"Yes, I do."

"Well, please don't go off like a rocket when I tell you your husband's an asshole. He's trying to manipulate you emotionally. He doesn't want a trial separation. He'll never leave you—he's got you exactly where he wants you. And now he's messing with your mind to make sure you stay there."

"He wouldn't do that. He loves me. And I love him."

I spoke loudly, aware that the words sounded hollow and that given my recent behavior, there was no reason for Nicholas to believe them. He didn't shoot my statement down in flames though, as I had feared he might.

Instead, he countered, "The word love is open to interpretation. And to abuse."

"You can't say that. You don't know him."

"I don't have to know him to have an opinion on him," Nicholas retorted, and the anger was back in his voice again.

"I don't have to listen to your opinion. Hey, where are we going?" I asked, as Nicholas turned off the main driveway and onto the track we had taken the day before.

"I'm going for a drive."

"But I…"

"You don't want to go?"

"No, I do, it's just…"

"Well, then. I need to go for a drive. I'd like for you to come along. Say no and I'll let you out now."

"You know I'm not going to say no." Damn it, I was smiling now, feeling as if a shaky equilibrium had been restored.

"I missed you last night," he said, driving carefully down a steeply sloping section of road, and I felt my stomach contract at his words.

"I'm sorry I didn't come back to your bedroom." I stared out of the window as the big truck eased carefully over a rocky section, while branches scraped lightly across its sides. What I had just said was an acknowledgement that things were not yet over between us. And why should they be, given that my husband and I were now facing the prospect of a trial separation?

"You had your reasons. I understand."

"I thought you were angry about it."

"No. I was disappointed, that's all."

"You seemed really pissed off this morning when I heard you in the gym."

"I was, but not with you."

"Do you always gym when you're pissed?"

"Mostly. It's a safe way of getting rid of it. And going for a drive is a good way of calming down."

As I pondered what he had said, I noticed the sky was beginning to clear and the sun was breaking through the clouds at last, brightening the morning. We drove past the place where we had fixed the fence the day before. After the rains last night, the river was flowing more rapidly through it, but no other trees had been uprooted or washed into the wires.

"I wouldn't have thought you would have much to be angry about," I said, thinking again of what it must be like to live in this utopia.

"Oh, trust me, Erin, I have plenty."

"What would an unsafe way be of handling it, then?"

"Of handling temper?"

"Yes."

"Taking it out on somebody else." His voice was hard, but it was his words that silenced me. Was he implying that this was what Vince had been doing?

Had Vince been doing this?

One thing I knew for sure was that, under normal circumstances, Vince's behavior would have had me frantic with worry. I would have been calling him every hour, thinking of little else, desperate to reassure him and to get our relationship back onto an even keel.

I hadn't done that, though.

Was that what was making Vince behave so weirdly?

"There!" Nicholas's voice interrupted my thoughts. He was pointing out of my window and looking in that direction, I saw a pair of rhino.

"Oh, wow," I breathed. The magnificent animals, their massive bodies a matte grey in color, their long, curved horns intact, were peacefully browsing some nearby bushes.

He stopped the car and for a few minutes we sat and watched them as they made their way across the dirt track before disappearing into an area of thicker bush.

"They're so beautiful," I breathed.

"Beautiful and endangered," Nicholas said sadly. The last remnants of the anger I'd sensed smoldering within him seemed to have dissipated. I felt calmer, too, the frayed emotions that I'd felt at Vince's words now soothed by the drive and this amazing sight.

"At least they're protected here."

"They're on my property," Nicholas agreed. "I'll do whatever it takes to keep them safe."

The passion with which he said the words made me glance at him in surprise. I didn't understand why, but I thought that the safety that Nicholas was striving so hard to uphold meant more than simply protecting the wildlife within his property's inner boundaries. Protecting his own was a matter that seemed to be deeply personal for him—but I could not guess at why.

"Here's the access gate that leads through into the main part of the estate, where the Big Five roam." He stopped the car by a wide gate that was closed and locked with a thick chain and padlock. "About a twenty-minute drive away from here is the most amazing place. It's a small wooden chalet, set on a hillside overlooking a dam. Occasionally, I spend one or two nights there; or just a lazy afternoon. I don't think I'll get the chance to take you there. I wish I could."

"Why don't we go now? Or have you got other things planned for today?"

He turned to stare at me and I was startled by the intensity in his eyes.

"We can go," he said slowly. "Even if I had plans, I'd put them aside for you."

He climbed out of the car and unlocked the gate. The chain clanked and rattled as the massive, heavy-duty padlock opened. Then he drove through, stopped the car again, and locked it once more behind him.

"I should warn you, just in case…" he said softly, and with a hint of embarrassment in his tone, "I'm out of condoms."

"Oh." Silently, I took in the implications of this statement.

"I'm not a risk, Erin. I have regular physicals before I travel to work in other countries, including blood tests. The most recent of those was in July this year. I don't know if you're on birth control, but if we end up making love, I will be careful, I promise." His voice was like a caress.

Making love? What happened to sex? To fucking? His choice of words was confusing me, although the desire that swept through me was not.

"I don't have any sexually transmitted diseases. I was tested for all of them recently," I told him. In fact, I'd had the tests done during one of Vince's jealous episodes. I'd hoped the results would set his mind at rest. They hadn't, of course.

"And I'm not on birth control," I added more slowly. "But you don't have to be careful in that regard."

He stared at me wide-eyed. "Why's that?"

I took a deep breath. "Long story."

"So, tell me the long story," he said. "I think it's time we learned more about each other."

"You've refused to tell me anything about yourself," I said.

"I know. I'm sorry. I'm bad that way. I promise to try, though."

Time to come clean with him, then. He might as well know what had happened to me to make me the person I was today.

"My little brother, Aidan, died when I was fourteen. It was such a shock—he was killed when a car went out of control. Two teenagers, drag racing. He was only ten years old at the time." I took a deep breath. "My mother went into a depression. She basically didn't leave the house for—oh, I don't know—two years, maybe. Those two years were hell. For me, and for my dad. He ended up divorcing her. Although maybe it's unfair to put it that way. Aidan's death led to them getting divorced."

"That must have been tough for you to cope with."

"It was. I coped by going off the rails. By the time I was sixteen I was out every night—my parents never knew where I was and if they had known, they would have forbidden me to go to those places. I went through a stage of doing drugs. I had a series of boyfriends. My longest relationship was with a man who was thirty years old, who'd been married and who'd fathered a child."

"Go on?" There was nothing but concern in Nicholas's tone. I could hear no disapproval. That was a relief. I hadn't gotten this far in my story when I'd tried to tell Vince. He'd been so judgmental when I mentioned the drugs, I'd thought it safer not to share the rest.

"Of course, I wasn't careful enough. I ended up having an ectopic pregnancy and didn't know until it ruptured. I had massive internal bleeding. I nearly died, and both my tubes were damaged so badly they had to remove them. If I were ever to have kids it would have to be through IVF, which might or might not work, and is not a prospect I'd be overly enthusiastic about in any case."

"I'm sorry to hear that." His face was serious. He moved his hand onto my leg and massaged it gently.

I shrugged, gave him a smile I didn't mean. "Shit happens."

"It does indeed."

I wasn't going to tell him that Vince had said, when we discussed this before we married, that he didn't want kids. But then, just a few weeks ago, he'd suddenly started criticizing me about being infertile, and had blamed me for the fact that he would never have a son.

Vince's words had left me feeling deeply insecure. But that was not something to speak about now. I really did not want to think any further about a topic which always made me feel angry and ashamed.

"My grades suffered as a result of all of this, of course," I told Nicholas. "I missed half of my final exams. I'd been planning on studying fine art, but in the end I had to settle for doing a photography course. I decided I needed to get away. From my family, my environment, the friends I'd lost. So I moved away and then I just kept going. Packing up and moving on became a habit."

"That must have been tough for you."

"It was my fault. I made some terrible decisions and I paid for them. I'm damaged goods now, and that is what…"

"No!" Nicholas just about shouted the word. He stopped the car and turned to face me, taking my hands in his own, and, surprised, I stared back at him. "Not damaged goods. Never. Don't ever say that, Erin."

"I—"

"Not unless you want to believe for the rest of your life that you're not good enough. And you know where that can lead." His voice was dark and I understood the warning behind it, even though it made me feel uncomfortable.

"There have been plenty of good times in my life, too," I said, making an effort to lighten the conversation.

"And in mine," Nicholas agreed, smiling slightly. "Present circumstances included."

I wanted to offer a casual agreement, but there was suddenly a lump in my throat that felt too big to swallow. I had been such an idiot. My decisions, in every way, had been so misguided, up to and including the ones I'd just made. Sleeping with this gorgeous man had been bad enough—but falling for him? And how on earth was I going to be able to leave him without leaving a piece of my heart behind?

We headed in silence down a track that became increasingly overgrown. Branches scraped against the sides of the car and the tires splashed through flooded ruts and ditches. The area was both incredibly beautiful and devastatingly wild. I felt at that moment, driving through that rough and lonely landscape, as if we might be the only two people in the world.

"It gives you a real sense of isolation, coming here," I said, wishing I could capture the sea of greenery, the empty sky with its towering clouds, in the eye of my camera lens.

"It does. It always makes me feel peaceful. I spend time here when I want to think."

Fifteen minutes later, he eased the car up a steep, winding road. I saw to my amazement that at the top of the hill was a small wooden chalet, built partly on long stilts and partly bermed into the hillside itself. Nicholas parked under the chalet and we climbed out.

"I'll go first," he said, walking around to a steep wooden staircase on the side of the building. "There is a tiny chance that there might be a stray scorpion in the bathroom, or another unwanted creature somewhere inside."

After that warning, I followed cautiously behind and waited outside the wooden door until he gave the all-clear.

Stepping inside, I caught my breath.

The small building smelled pleasantly of the mahogany boards that had been used in its construction. It had a surprisingly high, sloped roof and a simple layout. The main room, a bedroom, had a double bed positioned against the back wall and an enormous glazed window opposite. The window looked out over the sheer cliff-side onto the astonishing view below. Here, the azure waters of a large dam were spread out in front of us.

I caught my breath as I saw that, so close that I could make out every detail of their lithe, powerful bodies, a pride of five lions and two cubs were at the water's edge, drinking.

"Oh, wow!" I moved over to the window and stood, transfixed, watching this visual feast until the last of the lions had drunk their fill. Even then, the pride did not leave the dam area but instead moved to a shady spot of grass where they settled down to rest or, in the cubs' case, to play pouncing games with each other.

"It's amazing, isn't it?"

Nicholas's voice resonated from the room to the right of the bedroom, a kitchenette. Here, another door led out onto a small, shady balcony which also overlooked the dam. Nicholas was pouring water from a plastic jerry can into a kettle on a gas plate. A small gas-powered fridge stood by the window.

"The room opposite is a bathroom," he told me, pointing to the door. "Its water supply comes from a rainwater catchment tank on the roof."

When he made the coffee, I noticed there was only one mug on the wooden shelf.

"We'll have to share," Nicholas said. "You're the first person apart from me who's been in this hideaway since I had it built last year."

So he hadn't even brought Angela here? I felt illogically pleased to be the only one he'd shared this special hideaway with.

"Thank you for bringing me. It's incredible."

We sat down on the bed and leaned back on the cushions, passing the mug back and forth while staring out at the view of the endless sky and the grasslands and dam below. The peaceful sight soothed me and helped to calm my frazzled emotions. There was an extraordinary stillness in this place. The only sounds were of nature—insects, the calling of birds, the faint babble of water from somewhere nearby.

Nicholas was right—being part of this timeless, wild landscape was giving me the opportunity I required to think.

And I was thinking I needed to get back across that river fast.

Whatever this attraction was between us, I was prepared to admit that Nicholas was as much under its spell as I. While I was with him, the magnetism between us created a static that made it impossible to reason. Even now I could feel its tug—this ridiculous desire, this longing to touch him, this crazy feeling of happiness inside, of being at peace—as if everything had turned from impossibly complicated to utterly simple.

I told myself sternly that this was not real. It was an illusion of happiness. It could not last, and it was interfering with my perception of everything—including, most crucially, my own marriage.

I owed it to my husband to try and fix what had gone wrong between us. If my efforts did not work—and the idea of that happening made me feel disoriented, as if I were teetering on the edge of a tall building—then the foundations of my world would crumble.

I had to get out of here as soon as was humanly possible. This place—and this man—were becoming addictive. Nicholas and Leopard Rock Estate were drawing me in, making me forget that there was a world outside the borders and that I had a life I needed to go back to. I was becoming entangled, and this was not right, not healthy, and simply not acceptable.

I could not afford to let this happen. The next few days would be difficult enough. I needed to come to terms with what I had done, and try and fix my marriage. I would require all my strength of mind to get through this.

I handed the empty mug back to Nicholas and our fingers brushed. Quickly, I moved my hand away but he moved his toward me.

The touch interrupted my thoughts and distracted me from the task of shoring up my resolve. In any case, I told myself, I had made my decision. As soon as there was any way out of here—any way at all—I was going to take it. That would be within another two days at the most. In the meantime, I acknowledged reluctantly, I could not win the battle against my own desires. Besides, giving in to temptation would be all the sweeter now that I knew, for sure, there was so little time left for me to surrender.

CHAPTER 17

As our hands idly caressed, Nicholas' touch caused my heart to pound.

"This is something I've dreamt of doing for days. Bringing you here. Sharing this place with you."

He put the cup down and sprawled on the bed, pulling me close with one strong arm. His lips tasted of coffee and his kiss swiftly grew urgent. Only two more days at the most, I promised myself... and I must take every moment of pleasure they offered. In fact, I must saturate my senses with Nicholas de Lanoy in the hope that doing so would finally satisfy my craving for him.

His hands roamed over my body, stroking my breasts, teasing my nipples which stood out taut and hard under my shirt. He tugged at the fastening of my pants, and in turn, my fingers were at his jeans, unbuckling, unzipping, pulling them down, revealing him.

He made to remove my clothes, but I stopped him.

"No," I whispered. "Not yet." With the flat of my hand on his chest, I pushed him back onto the cushions, seeing the bewilderment in his eyes and feeling a sudden surge of power at having seized the moment, taken control for just a while of this powerful, magnificent man.

I kissed my way down his body, loving the silken sensation of his skin under my lips, the coarser tickle of hair, feeling the tension in him, the breathless anticipation of what I was about to do.

"Oh, Erin," he groaned as I wrapped my right hand around the pulsing length of his cock and flickered my tongue around its head. "God, that's good."

I could hear his breathing, rough and hard, and found I was breathless myself. I could feel his desire as if it was my own. I was trembling with excitement at his response. I longed to give him more; to take him to the same heights of bliss where he had taken me.

I opened my lips and slid them around the wide head of his cock, then circled the tip of my tongue slowly, lusciously around it, tasting him. I loved the feel of his skin, so silken soft compared to the powerful hardness underneath. I moved my lips further down his shaft, sucking him as deep as I could take him, caressing his thickness with my tongue. His helpless groans of delight made me feel incredibly aroused.

This was a sensual pleasure for me in a way I'd never felt it to be before, with other men... but, if I was truthful with myself, it was more than that. I was amazed by how much I needed to do this for him. I wanted to give him my all, to let him know the honesty of my desire, holding nothing back. It was as if, by pleasuring him so intimately, I was letting myself show the feelings I could never tell him.

After all... I had two more days at most before everything would remain unsaid forever.

I slid my lips rhythmically up and down his shaft, caressing him more firmly with my tongue, finding the pleasure points where he could not help but cry out as I massaged them, and where I felt him swell and throb in response to my touch.

"Oh, God, Erin, that feels so good. You must... you must stop now, or I'm going to..."

I disregarded his breathless instructions, loving that I was defying his wishes, sucking him hard and deep, wanting and needing to take him further than he had been taken before. His body tensed, his left hand closing around my left and grasping me hard as he let out a loud groan of pleasure. He felt hot in my mouth, as hard as granite, and then he gave himself up to me, spurting into my mouth, warm liquid, and I swallowed him greedily.

When I sat up he pulled me to him and kissed me long and hard. In the embrace of his strong arms I felt amazingly safe. With the taste of him still in my mouth, the feel of him next to me, my senses were filled by him and I was utterly at peace.

I closed my eyes as his breathing slowed, and when I opened them again it was to discover I'd fallen into a deep sleep. The light through the window was totally different—a bright reddish-gold of late afternoon.

Nicholas lay beside me. He was awake and reading a book. Peeking at the cover I saw it was a Stephen King novel. He seemed engrossed in it and I now realized the soft sound I'd heard while coming out of my sleep had been pages turning.

"Afternoon," he said, smoothing my hair away from my face. "You slept for hours. Take a look through the window. We have some more visitors."

Staring down at the dam, I caught my breath. A herd of four elephant had arrived at the water. They drank, then sluiced water over their massive, grey bodies with their trunks.

Nicholas laid his book aside and, in each other's arms, we watched their evening ritual. By the time the elephant had moved away, the sun was setting, blazing in through the window in a fiery mingling of colors.

"It's beautiful," I breathed.

"You're beautiful." He moved his hips against mine. I could feel him aroused once again, and realized I was breathless with desire for him. "Your eyes, Erin… they're incredible. The deepest blue I've ever seen. They sparkle when you smile. And I can't look at your lips without needing to kiss them." He brushed his mouth over mine.

"I want to see you naked," he murmured. "God, your body's a turn-on."

With careful fingers he unbuttoned my shirt before opening it.

"Your breasts… so firm, so round." He stroked his fingers gently over them before bending to suck and tease my nipples with his tongue. He nibbled at my left nipple before biting it harder, causing me to let out a small squeal at the unexpected sensation.

He ran his tongue over it again and heat spread through my body to pool in my core. Playful desire was escalating into urgent need. We both felt it—I could not deny it.

He slipped my shirt off and removed my pants.

I lay, staring up at his hard-muscled, aroused body as he knelt over me, taking me in with appreciative, admiring eyes. He was the beautiful one—a breathtakingly handsome man whose rugged appearance concealed the tantalizing complexity of character that lay beneath.

He ran his fingers lightly over my breastbone.

"I'm sorry I had to bruise you so badly."

"You were saving my life," I said, and gestured with my left hand to emphasize my words. The action caused the inside of my arm to be exposed and something inside me constricted as I saw his eyes narrow.

I tried to move my arm back again but he stopped me with a firm grasp on my wrist. He bent closer, examining the five telltale bruises which were fainter now than they had been, blurring purple-yellow, but still entirely visible.

"Erin," he said, and his voice was cold. "I didn't do that to you. I held you under your arms when I was dragging you out of the car. And this?" He ran his fingers lightly over the massive bruise on my hip.

I stared up at him, wordless, the fury I saw in his face making me feeling frightened even though I didn't know exactly why.

"Was that your husband?" he asked.

I found myself blinking tears away. I still couldn't speak. I gave a small nod.

"Jesus!" he snapped.

"It's not—it was just a moment when he lost his temper. He pulled me toward him and I banged my hip on something." My throat felt very dry. "It's never happened before."

"Don't lie to me," he said slowly. "It's happened before."

I shook my head, but the memories were flooding back now—Vince shaking me until my teeth rattled during a particularly vicious argument; Vince bending my finger back during a fight over possession of the remote control—he had meant to bend it, of course, had intended to cause me pain although he had certainly not meant to break it. I'd had to go to the emergency room and had spent six weeks in a splint.

Vince, enraged that I'd been speaking to another man at one of the launch parties for his new photographic collection, grabbing my arm as soon as we were in his apartment together, and forcing it back toward my face so hard and suddenly that my own hand had hit me with enough force to make my nose bleed.

I didn't know what to say to Nicholas now. I'd forgotten those incidents—or made myself forget—believing them or perhaps wanting them to be incidental, unimportant blips on the radar of Vince's and my relationship.

Silence filled the small chalet. Even the chorus of the birds outside seemed muted.

He exhaled deeply and let go of my wrist.

"It's never just once," he said again, more gently this time. "Not ever. Why didn't you tell me this had happened?"

"I didn't think it was such a big deal." My voice sounded very small.

"It's abuse," His voice was like steel.

"Well, not really, no. We just have a—a dynamic relationship."

"I'm sure that's how my parents' marriage started out as well," he said, in the coldest voice I had ever heard him use, and my eyes widened at the words. Was this what he had gone through? Was this the part of his past he did not want to talk about?

"Your parents?" I repeated, my voice unsteady.

"I can only surmise it escalated as the years went by. Nobody would marry a man they knew was going to put them in hospital once a month, would they?"

He stared down at me with icy eyes and I could find nothing to say in response.

"I'm sure that's how it started," he continued. "A pinch here. A slap there. Every time getting worse. Each time blaming the victim—because it's always your fault, isn't it, Erin? You should be schooled in that by now."

His voice was heavy with cynicism.

"By the time I was old enough to be aware of it, it had started in earnest. I'd lie in bed and listen to the punches. The meaty sound of flesh hitting flesh. My mother's screams. The way she'd beg and plead with him to stop. Sometimes she'd try to defend herself and then things inevitably got worse. Furniture would be knocked over. Glasses were smashed. The extent of his rage… it was uncontrollable. Brutal. And I grew up with it." He was blinking now—were those tears in his eyes?

"What did you do?" I asked softly.

"At first, when I was very young, I'd try to comfort my mother. To help her. Bring her ice. Stop the bleeding. Twice, I called the ambulance for her."

"Oh, Jesus, Nicholas, that's terrible."

"Later, I tried to intervene. I got smacked around for my troubles, although not as badly as he hit my older brother. For some reason, the abusive bastard didn't bother to hurt me, which made it all the worse. Then, a few years later, when I was bigger and stronger, I finally managed to best him. I put him on the floor with a black eye, two teeth missing, and concussion."

I didn't know what to say. I found his hand and held it, and he gripped mine tightly.

"God, Nicholas, I'm so sorry that had to happen to you. That you had to go through such a thing—with your own parents."

"It was hell," he told me, and looking into his eyes I could truly believe the words. I wanted to hold him, to offer him comfort from the agony he'd gone through, but when I reached for him, to pull him down beside me, he locked his arms around me and drew me up to sit facing him.

"Erin, I can't let this happen to you," he said slowly. "I can't. I don't even care to what degree it occurs. Abuse in any form is absolutely unacceptable. It is a crime."

"My situation is different, Nicholas. Vince is not a criminal. It's not abuse…"

"Your husband is a wife-beating bastard," he spat out.

"No!" I shouted. "Stop saying those things about him!"

Rage and shame flooded through me, so intense my eyes filled with tears. Seeing them, his face softened. "I'm sorry, Erin," he said, but when he tried to take me in his arms I pushed him away.

I was furious with myself for having let Nicholas see that bruise, and furious with him for having said these hurtful words. Instinctively, I had been trying to hide my arm from him, knowing deep down that he would say something if he saw it. The thought of Vince in jail for spousal abuse terrified me, so at that moment I could only defend my husband's actions. I was not like Nicholas's mother. I was not a victim, and never would be.

I was still seething when Nicholas got up and strode over to the window.

"Whatever, Erin. Believe what you like about him." His voice was filled with despair. "I can't convince you, even though you're a highly intelligent, independent-minded woman. You've got a blind spot when it comes to your self-worth. You're in denial. No matter what I say, it won't make a difference."

"With all due respect, Nicholas, I know Vince better than you do. He is not a violent man normally. Well, only when he gets upset with me, and I can control that. You went through hell, and so did your mother. That doesn't mean everyone who—who is in a physically passionate relationship is going to end up doing the same."

He didn't answer but simply shook his head. The distance between us felt suddenly huge and cold. I got out of bed and walked over to stand beside him, naked, locking my arms around him, staring through the window at the last fiery traces of the setting sun.

"Do you even hear your own words, Erin?" Nicholas asked quietly, staring out at the darkening landscape. "You blame yourself, just to make excuses for his appalling, out of control behavior."

"In a couple more days I'll be gone, Nicholas. You won't have to worry about me anymore, so why are you wasting time doing it now when we could be spending it so much more pleasurably?"

I smoothed my hands over his back. Then I locked my arms around him and kissed him.

At first, I felt him tense against me with anger, but then as my lips softened his, and his own parted, we melted into each other. Our tongues caressed, our bodies pressed tightly together. I felt the now-familiar rush of heat inside me, the incredible pulsing desire that his proximity triggered… and I knew that he was feeling it, too.

"Erin, how do you do this to me? It's crazy. Wonderful, but crazy," he whispered.

He walked the few steps to the bed and we fell on it together, kissing hard, almost frantically, as if both of us knew that this time might possibly be the last.

His lips trailed down my neck before he took my right nipple in his mouth, grazing it with his teeth before sliding his tongue over its hardening tip. I moaned softly, thrusting my hips toward him, the delight his touch offered triggering a more urgent, throbbing need in my lower belly.

"Such perfect, responsive nipples," he murmured, turning his attention to my left one, his pleasuring tautening a cord of desire inside me so intense that I thought I might come from this touch alone.

"Don't stop…" I managed, breathlessly, but he released my nipple, leaving it tight and hard.

He kissed his way down my body, his lips moving tenderly over my stomach and his tongue exploring my navel before trailing lower, and I caught my breath as he gently parted my legs to move between them. My clitoris throbbed so hard that I tensed, anticipating some discomfort when he touched it. I should have known better from the man who seemed to be able to read my mind… and my body.

He caressed it so softly and tenderly with his tongue that within moments I melted into the mattress. The exquisite, liquid stimulation this offered me was intensified when he slid two fingers into me, their tips gently massaging my G-spot. I was paralyzed by these caresses, a prisoner to my own delight, able only to clutch the sheet in my fingers as a storm of sensation brewed inside me.

I was breathing hard, my heart banging audibly, feeling myself quivering around him as the heat inside me overflowed. I came with an intensity that made me cry out, and his fingers stroked over the erogenous zones inside me to prolong and enhance my spasms of ecstasy.

What we were sharing was deeply, intensely sexual, but at the same time it was something more. I sensed there was a tenderness in his actions; an intimacy between us, that had not been present before.

"Erin," he breathed, moving over me to look into my eyes. His own pale eyes were wide and I could not read the expression in them, although I could feel the gentleness with which he kissed me. Now his cock was sliding deliciously over my wet, swollen outer lips and I wrapped my legs around him, angling myself to receive him.

"Are you okay with this?" he whispered, as the wide head of his cock touched my entrance, the caress causing me to catch my breath. He was asking, I knew, because this would be unprotected sex... and truly it felt like it, in more ways than one. I didn't have any defenses left against Nicholas. He had stripped them all away.

"I need you inside me," I told him. "I need to—to make love with you."

"I need to make love with you, too," he groaned. He cupped a hand under my buttocks and, in a series of deepening and utterly sensual thrusts, he entered me. All the while he stared into my eyes. I could not conceal the helpless pleasure that this full, naked penetration offered. He was pushing me wide open, filling me up with his hardness.

"You feel so good, Erin. My God, I'm touching you, inside you, naked." His voice was husky, filled with emotion.

I wrapped my arms around him, pressing myself close to him, feeling his powerfully muscled back and the rhythmic flexing of his buttocks as he drove himself into me. Slowing his rhythm, he eased himself out before pushing in slowly again and again, letting his thickness glide over all my most sensitive points so that I moaned with the pleasure of it. I felt so in harmony with him, as if we were truly one... the closeness was astonishing and I found myself having to bite back words that I could not risk saying aloud.

Better to think of the sex—to focus on the sheer, raw physical pleasure of this act. Every nerve ending in my body was sparking with delight at his slow, deliberate movements. My eyes were locked with his and I felt as if I was drowning in his gaze.

"And now we go harder," he whispered, angling his pelvis and withdrawing almost all the way before spearing into me so brutally deep and hard that my eyes widened and I braced myself, anticipating that this would be painful. But as he reached the deepest point, he slowed, easing himself in to fill me completely, so that his engorged head softly kissed my most tender depths.

"Don't worry," he murmured, his fingers stroking and teasing my throbbing nipples. "I don't ever want to hurt you. I want to take you. To become one with you. No resistance... no boundaries."

"Oh, God, that's good," I gasped, as he pushed into me again and again. The sensation was incredible. With me totally relaxed, completely trusting, he was able to slowly increase the tempo and vigor of his deep thrusts while offering me one of the most erotic and intimate experiences I had ever had.

I was opened to him, vulnerable to him, completely possessed by him, and it was so astonishingly sexy. I'd never believed I could orgasm in this position, in this way, but my body knew better. I felt my pleasure ratcheting up to a level that was making me breathe fast and thrust my hips toward him. In his eyes, I saw my own amazed delight reflected.

"Yes," he encouraged me. His fast, powerful movements were filling me up, I was taking him all, as deep as he could go, and the sensation was exquisite. I was gasping, sweat suddenly turning my skin warm and slick, and suddenly it was too much. The friction was so unbearably delicious it was sending me into a place I'd never been before.

Wild with need, I clawed my fingers into his shoulders, shoving my pelvis into his, bruising my clitoris against him as I greedily devoured the ravishment I needed to reach the final summit. God, his thrusts were turning my G-spot into a liquid hot erogenous zone. I was tightening, quivering, I could not help crying out. I saw his eyes narrow, his face slacken, as he watched me come undone.

My orgasm shook me to my foundations. I came painfully hard, digging my nails into his skin as the convulsions of delight shook my body. And then, as if he'd only just been able to retain the control he needed to see me satisfied, he rammed himself into me once more with a breathless groan. Deep inside, I could feel every powerful spurt that he pumped into me.

My heart was pounding; my body trembling. I did not think I would be able to move for a long while—years, perhaps. Nicholas was still inside me, holding me tightly, soothing my rapid breathing with gentle kisses and whispered endearments so loving they tore at my heart.

Even as I held him in my arms, tasting his skin with my lips and feeling the liquid heat of him inside me, I was doing my best to break free from these wicked tendrils of longing that were drawing me to him again.

After all, this lovemaking could well have been our last. As phenomenal a lover as Nicholas was, and as tender as his words to me were, by the time I was able to leave I was sure he would be tiring of me, ready for some more solitude before his next depraved foray into the world of married women.

And it was best I did not think of where I would be going, or what I would be doing.

CHAPTER 18

IT WAS FULLY DARK by the time we got up. We dressed by the light of a gas lamp, and Nicholas shone a flashlight out of the doorway, helping me down the steep ladder-like staircase and back to the car. We drove back to the lodge in companionable silence, going slowly, with the window half open and the orchestra of night sounds filtering into the car.

"Let's see what Miriam left for us," Nicholas said, slamming the car door and waiting for me to get out before we headed through to the kitchen. "I don't know about you, Erin, but I'm absolutely starving. And it's all your fault." He shot me an unapologetic grin.

The clock on the wall told me it was eight-thirty p.m. and I realized I too was famished.

"We're in luck," he announced from behind the open refrigerator door. "There's a venison pie here, and coleslaw. Do you want a glass of wine?"

A few minutes later we'd assembled our meal at the kitchen table and placed the pie in the oven to heat up. We sat at the table and I downed a full glass of water in a few gulps, realizing I was as thirsty as I was hungry. Nicholas refilled it, and I drank the next one more slowly before starting on my wine.

Nicholas checked his phone, which he'd left in the truck for the day, and listened to his messages. While he was doing that, I took the opportunity to check mine.

Vince had called three times and left no messages. Still, three phone calls was a lot for a man whose most recent words to me had been that he wanted a trial separation. I could only pray he'd reconsidered. I would call him first thing tomorrow, I decided.

Nicholas disconnected and put his phone away.

"They've repaired the dam," he told me. "Joshua says that by the day after tomorrow the new temporary bridge will definitely be passable for pedestrians, possibly even for vehicles. And the police called to say they're wrapping up the search and rescue operation tomorrow—the one they were using my helicopter to help with. They've been able to restore the community's access to the outside world and transport the survivors safely to hospital."

"I'm so relieved to hear that."

The kitchen was filling with the delicious aroma of warming gravy and crisping pastry. Nicholas took the pie out of the oven and cut us each an enormous slice, while I heaped coleslaw onto the plates. This, then, was the second to last night I would ever spend in his company, conversing with him, making love, eating the food carefully prepared by knowledgeable staff.

"I can't thank you enough for everything," I said.

He frowned at me, genuinely puzzled. "For what?"

"For putting me up here—hell, for putting up with me here." I laughed, and he gave a rather reluctant smile. "For making this time so special. Oh, and not least, for saving my life."

He didn't look pleased at that, but instead gave a small shrug and began eating.

I felt there was more to be said about what we'd discussed earlier that afternoon, and now seemed like a good time for me to broach a sensitive topic.

"Thank you for telling me about your home life when you were younger," I said. "It's helped me understand you better."

"I'm glad it has."

It was true. Knowing that Nicholas came from an abusive background had helped me figure out a lot about him. His decision to become a paramedic, to help other people in need. His desire to protect people and animals in his care. His need to safely channel his own anger into intense physical exertion.

"Can I ask you something else?"

"Of course you can." He sounded wary, though.

"What was he like? Your dad, I mean. What made him do what he did?"

Nicholas took a long time to think about his answer.

"If you'd met him on the street or in the boardroom you'd never have known the real person," he said. "He was a well-educated man, and he could be very charming. Deep down, though, he was a bastard. A cold-hearted bastard with a terrible temper. He had no conscience, either in business or at home. He was psychopathic, I think, although he hid it well."

"I'd imagined him as—as somehow being less educated."

Nicholas's grim head-shake told me how wrong I was. "It's not only uneducated people who are abusive. Although it made it worse, in a way, that he wasn't just some dumb redneck who'd drink his salary every week and then come home and cause hell. My father was a highly qualified man and he became a billionaire through his own cunning, even though I did not approve of his methods."

"What did he do?" I asked.

Nicholas piled a second helping onto both our plates and refilled our wineglasses.

"My father made his money by loaning capital to struggling companies, buying a controlling interest in them, and basically raping them with crippling interest rates and payback terms for as many years as he could. They often ended up going under after he'd made a massive profit. If they survived, he'd sell them to their competitors."

"That's so destructive!"

He nodded. "He toasted their suffering with Tanqueray. And my mother just wouldn't leave him, Erin. She was too damned traditional, or loyal, for her own good. No matter how hard I tried to persuade her, no matter how many times he threatened her with divorce, she would not walk out of that marriage."

I stared at Nicholas, and saw sadness in his eyes. I understood now his preference for no-strings-attached relationships.

"Are they still married?"

"They're both dead," Nicholas replied baldly. "My mother died first. Until her death, my father continued to beat and abuse her, so to escape her situation, she began drinking heavily. That habit started while I was still at boarding school. In the end, she passed away from liver cancer."

I shook my head. I didn't know what to say to that. We continued eating in silence, and I felt a heavy depression descending on me. I felt as if I was only just beginning to know the truth of this man—now, too late, when I was about to leave. Nicholas de Lanoy was no longer the womanizing rogue I'd thought him to be when we first met. I now understood he was a far more complicated human being, a loner, a man who had been afraid to put down roots. Nicholas was a courageous person who had fought his own personal battles and still, from time to time, was forced to conquer his inner demons.

With a sense of unreality, I realized that, fundamentally, Nicholas was far more like me than I'd first presumed.

Our meal finished, he reached across the table and took my hand.

"Will you spend the night with me, Erin?"

It was odd how that single, simple request captured my emotions. After all, it might be the only remaining chance to be with him.

"Of course I will."

"Come on, then."

❖ ❖ ❖

We took a long shower together, kissing deeply under the steaming cascade of water and soaping each other's bodies before stepping out into the embrace of his enormous fluffy towels. A few minutes later, we were in bed, with music playing softly in the background and a box of Ferrero Rocher chocolates on the pillow between us. We each had a book in our hand, but interrupted our reading from time to time to speak about whatever topics came to mind. My legs were draped over Nicholas's, and he was stroking my thighs lightly with his fingers while he read.

"I could get used to doing this," he remarked. "Erin, I don't think I'm going to be able to let you go. Bridge or no bridge, you're going to have to stay with me."

"I'll take that as a compliment," I said, keeping my voice deliberately light.

"It's more than that."

"Do you...?" I asked, looking up from my book, and then suddenly wished I hadn't broached such a personal subject.

"Do I what?"

"Do you do this with all your lovers?"

"What, this? Like we are now?"

"Yes."

"No," he said shortly. And then, as if trying to explain himself, "I've had quite an isolated life so far, Erin, in terms of personal relationships at least. Partly due to my family life growing up, and partly due to my choice of career."

"Tell me about your career," I said, suddenly needing to know about this piece in the puzzle of Nicholas' past.

"I trained as a paramedic when I'd finished school. My father wanted me to go to university but instead I joined the army, and later worked for other organizations, doing assignments in high risk areas and war zones."

"Oh." I nodded, understanding his loner lifestyle.

"I've made good money, more than enough to live comfortably, although you couldn't ever compare my earnings to my father's rotten billions. But then, three years ago, he died, and I found he'd left every penny of his inheritance to me. I never expected it. I was working up in Libya at the time. I came home and found myself the owner of a fortune I didn't want."

"What about your brother?"

Nicholas's lips tightened. "My father wasn't the only vicious bastard in our family. My brother grew up worse than him. He's in prison now, serving a life sentence. And trust me, you don't want to know what it's for."

"You're right, I don't." I said, feeling suddenly cold.

"My immediate family members are, or were, a violent psychopath, an alcoholic, and a cold-blooded criminal. I might have managed to escape those flawed genes by some miracle, but I am certainly not risking passing them on. Not ever. The de Lanoy family name will die with me. I will never have children of my own—and I consider that my service to humanity."

His voice was as hard as his face. I did not doubt the sincerity of his words. For a moment I reflected on the strange coincidence that he did not want children while I could not have them.

Perhaps, in another lifetime... if fate had brought us together... but that was seductive thinking and I must not pursue it. It was hard enough for me to cope with the painful reality that, one day, some other woman—I now realized, some extremely lucky woman—would be Nicholas's life partner when he was finally ready to settle down.

Choosing a safer line of questioning, I asked, "Did you buy this place when you inherited your father's money?"

"Yes. I needed somewhere to live and this was on the market, complete with all its furnishings and fittings as well as its staff. I thought it would be a good place to stay while I decided what to do with the inheritance."

"And what did you do?"

"At first I wanted to give all of it away—I believed it was blood money, earned through destructive means. But after some consideration, I decided instead to put it to better use."

"What use?"

"I have put the entire capital sum in a high yield portfolio. Then the interest—which is about a quarter of a billion each year—I've been using to start up and grow businesses that make a difference. I've invested in ventures that help people to help others, and teach people skills. I want to try to make up for what my father destroyed. I didn't know much about business and still don't, but I've taken some good advice from experts, and hired a financial manager who knows what he's doing, and so far most of the projects I've supported have shown growth. At worst, they've enabled people to earn a good living and become self-sufficient, and that makes me feel better about keeping the inheritance."

"That's awesome," I said, and he smiled.

"I'm glad you think so." He stroked my face tenderly before returning his attention to his book.

Let me not be clingy or tearful when the time comes, I caught my breath. *Let me be able to turn my back on this beautiful man and see this love affair for what it is.*

After all, what was it, really? A week of sinful pleasure that served to teach me that my moral standards were nowhere near as high as I had believed them to be.

And, please, let me not end up falling in love with him, I prayed, although I feared my prayers were already too late.

⚜ ⚜ ⚜

Much later I woke, disoriented, from a deep slumber. Tangled in the residue of forgotten dreams, I took a moment to remember where I was. In Nicholas's bed—but after making love and falling asleep in his arms, I now sensed that I was alone.

A quick exploration with my left hand confirmed the fact that the other side of the bed was empty, the sheets cool, the covers rumpled.

Puzzled, and now awake, I sat up, wondering where Nicholas had gone. Straining my ears, I thought I could hear the low murmur of his voice. For some reason, thinking of him having a whispered, night time conversation sent a chill of unease through me. Was something wrong?

Slipping on the silk robe I'd found in the bathroom, I padded out of the room to see if I could find him.

The sound of his voice became clearer as I walked softly down the passage. Before I rounded the corner I could make out what he was saying.

"That's fine. I'll be out there in twenty minutes." He paused. "No, I can't make it sooner. I'll need another spotter, and I will have to call my…"

He broke off as I walked round the corner.

"Okay. See you then," he finished abruptly.

"Hey," I said softly. "Is anything wrong?"

"Yes." He moved over to me, put an arm around me, kissed me. "I didn't want to disturb you, but I'm going to have to go out now."

"Out? Where? And why?"

"A gang of poachers just tried to kill one of the white rhino in Kruger Park. There was a shoot-out and they fled on foot, in the direction of our boundary fence. I'm going to call Joshua now, and we're going to go out and see if we can spot them. The rangers can't use their vehicles because of the flooding on that side, so it's important we get there fast."

I thought about this for a moment.

"You said if you call Joshua, there will be a delay."

"Yes. His house is on the other side of the estate, about ten minutes' drive from here."

"Well, take me along, then," I said, with more bravado than I felt. "Ready in two minutes, and then we'll bag these guys."

Nicholas gave me a reluctant smile. "Sorry, Erin, I'm not exposing you to this danger."

"Why not?"

"It could get violent. The gang is armed. You'll be safe here with all the doors locked."

"Hey, I'm already living on borrowed time. I'd be dead now if it wasn't for you."

Striding back toward the bedroom, he gave me another tight smile, "Even so, I can't let you come along, and that's the end of it."

"You can't stop me," I retorted. "And that's the truth of it. Remember, I've got a good eye for seeing things in the bush. Your words, Nicholas!"

"It's going to be too dangerous," he insisted.

"I'm a photographer. I've taken footage of violent urban riots, and forest fires, and natural disasters. Danger is part of my job. I might not have my camera with me, but if I did, I'd be coming with you and bringing it along."

I turned on the light and pulled on my clothes. I slipped my feet into my too-big borrowed sandals, and I was ready to go before Nicholas had fastened his own combat boots.

He stared at me with a blend of frustration and admiration. Raising my chin, I stared back at him, trying as hard as I could to give the impression of a tough woman who knew exactly what she was doing.

"All right," he said. "Let's get moving."

He took his Remington out of the safe in his bedroom. As we hurried out to the garage, he got on the phone to Joshua and told him to drive up to the boundary as soon as he could. Then we bundled ourselves into the truck and set off into the moonless night.

"I've got a spotlight here which I'll use if I need to," Nicholas told me in a quiet voice. "For now, though, you just need to try and get your eyes accustomed to how the bush looks at night. These poachers will keep still when they see our headlights. It won't be easy to pick them out because they'll be wearing neutral colors, to blend with their surroundings."

"No worries. We'll spot 'em." I could hear the nervousness in my own voice. It wasn't only the fact that this was a potentially dangerous situation—it was also that I really did not want to let Nicholas down. He'd trusted me enough to bring me with him—and now I needed to prove myself to him.

"Scout for loose wires in case they've broken through to this side," he said. "Probably, though, they'll be hiding out near the boundary on the Kruger Park side, waiting for another chance to go back in and track the rhino. So we'll go through the gate and start hunting on that side of the fence."

Oh, boy. And there I was thinking we'd be staying safely on our side of the fence and peering through. My stomach twisted. I took a deep breath and tried to think of the rhino, the magnificent animals whose lives would be saved.

The portable radio crackled and Nicholas answered it, communicating with the rangers who were on their way, and were to be backed up by a helicopter from the South African police service.

"Looks like there'll be a lot of backup arriving soon," he reassured me, putting down the radio speaker and shifting to low gear to accelerate up a hill. The Land Cruiser rocked and swayed as it hurtled along the dark tracks. Branches scraped the sides of the car and every so often I heard a loud popping noise as a stone flew out from under the tires. Once, I saw a flurry of retreating backsides as a herd of impala ran to escape the noisy threat of our vehicle, and I also noticed the pale fluttering of wings as a large bird—an owl, perhaps—took off from a nearby tree.

"Let's hope the backup arrives in time," I said nervously.

"Let's hope it does."

Nicholas skidded to a stop at the gate and dragged it open before driving through. He then got out and padlocked it firmly behind him again. No poacher would be sneaking through this entrance to prey on his beloved black rhino.

"We'll start south," he said, climbing back in the truck. "The poachers would have been coming from that side of the park, according to what the rangers said. With some luck, we'll intercept them."

The bush looked so different at night. The truck's lights threw the trees and bushes into sharp, uncompromising relief. In the harsh bright headlights, the muted greens and golds of the veld had morphed into subdued grays, sooty blacks, and bright, blinding whites.

Narrowing my eyes, I stared into the tangle of brush and undergrowth. Surely they would not hide near a road—but then again, in the darkness, perhaps they did not know where all the roads were. Certainly they would not be standing up. I needed to keep my eyes down, where the vegetation was thickest, looking for any signs of a human being—without being misled by a rock, or a twisted branch, or stump.

"Take the light, Erin," Nicholas told me, and I grasped the large spotlight before buzzing the window down and hooking it over the side of the door. I noticed that he had his rifle at the ready, its muzzle jutting out of his open window. He was driving slowly now, easing his way along the road, giving us both plenty of time to take in what lay on either side.

Shoot first…

As a photographer I knew the saying all too well, even though my interpretation of the phrase had involved a shutter and a lens rather than bullets and a gun.

The spotlight was intensely bright and penetrated deep into the undergrowth, but it produced a confusion of shadows and shapes. More than once I drew breath, ready to tell Nicholas to stop, but each time whatever I was looking at resolved itself into a natural and unsuspicious form. It struck me powerfully that this issue was bigger than affairs or infidelity—this was a matter of life and death, good against evil, a hellish battle playing out in what I had perceived to be paradise.

We traveled for another ten minutes before I saw the movement in the undergrowth.

It was such a tiny motion, a slow downward easing of a shadow, and the only reason I noticed it was that the night was otherwise so perfectly still. I strained my eyes but could see nothing more… all the same, what could have caused it? An animal would have moved fast, bursting out of the undergrowth.

"Nicholas," I said in a low voice. "I saw something there, on the left."

"Where?" His voice was soft but urgent. He stopped the vehicle and leaned across to stare out of my window.

"Just beyond that taller bush, the one straight ahead." I pointed. "You can't see it now, but there was a movement there."

Nicholas eased the truck backwards a few yards and then we caught our breath simultaneously as we both saw it through a clearing in the grass. An unmistakably human form, lying prostrate on the ground.

He got onto his cell phone, I supposed because it was quieter than the crackling radio, and within seconds was speaking in a low voice to the game rangers.

"We've got at least one of them here, possibly others," he said. "Hiding out about twenty yards east of where we are on the road." He gave the ranger the exact coordinates. "How far away are you?"

He listened, then spoke again. "Okay. We'll stay here and watch them. We'll see straight away if they try to move." He paused. "Good. In five, then."

"The rangers are five minutes away," he whispered. "They're going to walk up a parallel track, then head toward us from the western side and hopefully bracket the poachers. Just be careful, Erin. There's a chance these guys may panic and try to shoot their way out of here. Any gunfire, and you get down, okay?"

"Yes," I murmured, and swallowed, my mouth suddenly dry.

Five minutes had never passed so slowly, nor seemed to race by so fast. The poacher, or poachers, must suspect that we had spotted them because we were stopped nearby. Why were they still laying low? Were they, too, making frantic contingency plans in the same way we were? I supposed that with the powerful spotlight blinding them, they didn't have many options but to stay where they were, cowering face down in the muddy soil.

Suddenly, another brilliant flashlight illuminated the bush from a point beyond the poachers. Over a crackling megaphone, a loud voice demanded the criminals' surrender.

"Give yourselves up! Put your weapons down immediately. Hands in the air!"

I tensed as gunfire exploded around us. In a split-second, Nicholas had shoved me down onto the seat.

He leaned over me, protecting my body with his own as he flattened his foot on the gas pedal. The engine roared and we followed a haphazard route along the track, with the big vehicle swaying and jouncing. He must be finding it difficult to steer, I thought dazedly, since I could still feel his body over mine. Or was there another reason for his erratic driving? Surely—surely—he could not have been hit?

As the Land Cruiser finally skidded to a stop, my heart raced with anxiety at the thought of Nicholas wounded. I was desperate to confirm he was unhurt. Was it safe to speak now? Surely it must be.

"Nicholas?" I whispered.

"Erin?

"You okay?"

"Keep down for now. I'm fine. You okay?"

As I said, "Yes," another deafening round of gunfire broke out. Then silence my ringing eardrums couldn't register. Soon, it was broken by shouts, a scream and a groan, and another, louder noise I recognized—the sound of a helicopter.

"That's the police," Nicholas said, straightening up. That crazy, zigzag drive had taken us a long way down the track. One of the rangers, his clothes wet and streaked with mud, stood on a flat section of the road with a flashlight, guiding the helicopter down.

Nicholas let out a deep breath. Then he reached for me and held me tightly in his arms.

"That was a very close call. We could easily have been hit. Thank God you're all right. Thank God."

"Well, you're the one who got us out of the way," I stammered. I was shaking uncontrollably. I wanted to say thank God that he was unhurt.

Slowly, Nicholas reversed toward the scene and climbed out. "Stay in the truck until I say otherwise," he cautioned me, before striding toward the group gathered some distance away.

A minute later, I heard him calling.

"Erin! Could you come along and bring my first aid kit? The box in the back."

Oh, Jesus, we'd been lucky, but somebody was wounded.

I scrambled out of the car and snatched the heavy box out of the back before jogging over to the group. The four poachers lay face down in the mud, their khaki outfits slathered in grime. Their hands were cuffed behind them and one ranger stood over them, his Kalashnikov pointed at the prisoners. A mud-spattered armory of confiscated weapons and tools was strewn on the ground a short distance away.

Nicholas bent over a fifth man who lay on his back, groaning, while another ranger trained a flashlight on them. In the bright light I could see the crimson stream of blood spurting from his drenched khaki leg. The man's face looked Asian… Surprised, I realized the injured man was one of the poachers.

"Thanks," Nicholas said to me. He opened up the box and snapped on a pair of surgical gloves. I crouched down beside him and passed him equipment as he asked for it.

"He gonna die?" the ranger asked, his tone implying that he didn't really care. For one fierce moment, I couldn't help sympathizing with his viewpoint. After all, shots had been fired from both sides, and if the poachers' aim had been better, it could now be one of the rangers bleeding on the ground.

"Bullet hit his thigh," Nicholas said to the ranger. "Quick, Erin, scissors! And the gauze." He worked swiftly and in silence for a minute before adding, "Just missed the femoral artery, but it's ruptured a major vein. I suspect the bone's broken if not shattered. I'll get the bleeding under control, but he'll need hospital fast!"

Carefully, Nicholas cut the man's bloodied trouser leg away.

"Police are here now," the ranger observed. "They can fly him to hospital. Be nice if he survived," he added with heavy humor. "The others told us he's the ringleader so he'll have all the intel."

The poacher stared blankly up at Nicholas, biting his lip in pain as his wounds were attended to. His face looked drawn with shock, and his eyes were shadowed. I wondered whether he would survive, and if he did, whether he would keep his leg. Either way, I was glad the rhino were safe for now. I watched, feeling dazed by the trauma of the night's events, as the three armed policemen interviewed the rangers and took photographs of the scene.

"Erin," Nicholas said to me in a gentle voice once he'd finished stabilizing the injured man, "I'm going to have to fly out with the police, and accompany this patient to Hoedspruit hospital. That means

I'll be home tomorrow. Joshua should arrive any minute. When he does, could you follow him back to the lodge in my car? He'll stay there with you until Miriam arrives."

Nicholas—leaving? I felt stricken at the thought, and he must have seen my expression change because he added, "I'll get a ride to the Nelspruit police headquarters tomorrow morning, and fly my own helicopter from there back to Leopard Rock."

"Ready?" one of the rangers asked.

"Ja," the other agreed. In a strong Afrikaans accent, he continued, "There's a police van on the way to meet us on the other side of the floods."

Accompanied by two of the policemen, the handcuffed rhino poachers were escorted the way they had come, in convoy with the rangers. Nicholas and the third policeman strapped the injured man to a makeshift stretcher and lifted him into the helicopter. And then, just as the lights of Joshua's vehicle appeared over the hill, Nicholas approached me. He looked exhausted, and his gloves and sleeves were spattered with blood to the elbow. Leaning forward, he kissed me gently.

I felt tears stinging my eyes. Nicholas must never guess the truth of my feelings for him. It was going to be hard enough saying goodbye to this man—but dealing with his compassion would be unbearable.

"I'll see you tomorrow," he said. "Please, Erin…"

He didn't finish what he was saying. Instead, with a shake of his head, he climbed quickly into the helicopter. A minute later, they were airborne and out of sight.

I got into the driver's seat of the Land Cruiser. The seat was too far back and I had to adjust it forward to reach the pedals. Then, following Joshua, I drove slowly back down the hill toward the estate, noticing that the first faint light of the rising sun was brightening the horizon.

This would be the first day I would spend without Nicholas at Leopard Rock, and I could not help wondering, with a twinge of anxiety, what it would bring.

CHAPTER 19

JOSHUA DROVE THE WHOLE way back behind me and despite my reassurances that I would be fine, he waited at the lodge until Miriam and the other staff arrived. Despite his presence, I was aware of how silent the place was, how loud my footsteps sounded on the shiny tiled floor.

I did not go into Nicholas's bedroom. I felt strangely reluctant to do so—as if I had no right to walk in there on my own, to see the bed with its sheets still crumpled from the hours we had spent together.

Instead, I went back to my room and turned on my phone. As I waited for it to power up and find a signal, my resolve crystallized.

I was going to accept Vince's proposal for the trial separation. Given the cracks our relationship had shown over the past few days, I felt my husband had a valid point. We both needed a chance to think things through—although how spending more time apart was going to help our marriage, I wasn't sure. Perhaps counseling was the answer. We needed to develop better coping structures for communicating, to avoid the inevitable arguments. Getting Vince to agree to counseling might be tricky, though, because I knew he would consider it a sign of failure.

Suddenly and fervently, I wished that the damned bridge had never been washed away. That, instead, I'd ended up at the hotel with Vince that afternoon, where I could have apologized and we would have been able to make up. We would never have gone through the issues, the bitterness, that had been caused by our enforced separation.

I would never have been tempted by Nicholas. I would never have betrayed my husband.

I took a deep breath but my chest suddenly felt tight. My hands were cold. I sank down onto the chair, feeling physically crushed by the weight of my guilt.

This was it—the moment I had been expecting and dreading. With Nicholas gone, I had no defense against the onslaught of emotion that battered me.

Feeling nauseous, I rested my head on my folded arms, tears squeezing their way from out of my tightly shut eyes. I stayed like that for a few minutes, paralyzed by the intensity of my regret.

I'd only just started to struggle for coherence, to try and plan what on earth my next step should be, when my thoughts were interrupted by the loud ringing of my borrowed phone.

A sense of doom settled on me as I saw Vince's number on the line. I didn't want to answer, but I forced myself to press the connect button and take the call.

"Hey, hon," I said, realizing how tired my voice sounded.

"Hey, hon."

My eyes widened as I heard the gentleness in his words.

"How're you doing?" he continued.

"I... I'm fine. You're calling early. Is everything okay?"

"I'm not okay," he said. "I'm missing you, baby. I just wanted to tell you."

I let out a long breath. He hadn't mentioned the trial separation, nor made any accusations. This was the old Vince back again—the man I knew, the man I loved. The sharpness was gone from his voice; the edge of anxiety and distrust was no longer there. This was the man who had put his arms around me the first time he'd invited me back to his apartment, nuzzling my neck as we stared out of the window together at the shimmering Manhattan skyline. This was the man who had patiently spent an entire day shopping with me and who had paid for a new wardrobe at Bergdorf, Goodman, Bendel's, and Chanel, one that would improve my image and reflect my beauty, he had said. This was the man who liked to make love in front of a mirror—so he could watch us both from every angle.

This was the man who had enslaved me, captivated me, swept me off my feet. Who had proposed to me. Asked me—invited me—implored me to spend my life with him. My life... not six salacious days of love-shack.

Now the tears were streaming down my cheeks. I needed to get back to Vince, and do so now, while everything was good between us, before it could all go wrong again.

"I'm missing you, too," I said. "Vince, the bridge has been partway rebuilt. It isn't totally safe yet, but I can wade the part that's not sandbagged, I think. I'm going to walk down there now. Please meet me. Can you find your way? You should remember the road, right?"

"Baby, are you sure?" Vince asked. "I don't want you putting yourself in danger for me."

"I'm sure. I can't wait any longer."

"If you can't wait, I'll come and get you. I'll be there in an hour and a half."

This was the Vince I wanted back. Upbeat and positive, not stewing in jealousy. He was going to come and get me. In an hour and a half, I could have my life back. I could be taking the first step to be free of this debilitating guilt that was made all the more intense knowing that on this side, my bridges were already burned. Even if Vince had refused to see me ever again, staying with Nicholas would not be an option. Telling Nicholas how I felt about him would never be possible. Falling in love with Nicholas would be a huge, heartbreaking mistake and the thought of it happening was making me feel very afraid. Compared to this, my shaky marriage seemed like a refuge.

"I'll be there, Vince," I said.

I dressed quickly in my own clothes, the ones I'd been wearing when I had drowned. I needed shoes, though, so I took the pair of too-big sandals. I left behind me the computer and, after some thought, the cell phone too.

I paused for a long moment deciding what I should say to Nicholas. In the end I wrote a brief note in the book he'd provided for me.

Hi Nicholas. I'm going back over the bridge this morning. Thank you for saving my life, and I will never forget your generous hospitality.

I wanted to add something personal, to tell him what this time had really meant to me, but I did not know what to write. Staring down at the paper, I was swamped with depression, as if by leaving Leopard Rock, I would be leaving an essential part of my life—of myself—behind me. But I wasn't, of course. I was going back to what was important, and I was leaving behind me nothing more than a short week which Nicholas, and I hoped I, would swiftly forget.

Anyway, better not to dwell on that now. Not when I needed to get going. I didn't want to go back into Nicholas's bedroom. I could not.

I left the book on the desk in my bedroom and hurried down the passage and out of the front door before making my way at a slow jog, in the early morning light, down the paved driveway. As I pushed the main gate of the estate closed behind me and set off on the long walk down to the river, I tried to focus on what lay ahead, and did my best to endure the welling pain of knowing I was turning my back on Nicholas forever.

✢ ✢ ✢

The steel girders that had been laid across the river banks had seemed more solid yesterday than they did now. There were only two of them, each only a few inches wide and placed a foot apart. They looked flimsy against the vast expanse of rapids and they seemed only just to reach the sandbagged portion of the far bank. A few yards below, the river looked shallower now, but was still flowing fiercely. I noted with a twist of my stomach that some of the sandbags below the girders had been washed away. Hopefully, the upper ones would hold.

I took a deep breath. Changing my mind now was impossible. This had to be done. I slipped and slid my way down the sandbags and managed to bash my toe against the edge of the girder. Cursing softly, I rubbed it before wedging my feet against the slick surface of the bags and staring down at the metal, covered in condensation and, up close, looking even more treacherous. I slipped my sandals off, hoping I would have better grip with bare feet.

Clutching the side of the bank with my mud-streaked hand, I reached tentatively forward with my right foot and placed it on the steel support.

Yup—it was as slippery as I'd feared, and my bare feet offered frighteningly little traction. Even with one foot on each of the girders, I was not able to shuffle my way along. The risk of falling in the river was too great.

Only one thing to do then. I put my sandals down. To get over this river safely, I'd have to leave them behind. Letting go of my handhold, I lowered myself onto my knees and grabbed the metal bars with my outstretched hands. I would crawl across if I had to—if it meant that I would have a chance of reaching the other side.

The girders were surprisingly cold; their surface stained in places by patchy rust whose ragged edges sliced into my palms as I crawled. I put one hand forward, then the other. Then I slid my knees along to follow. I could do it this way as long as I concentrated and kept my focus. As long as I didn't lose my balance, get vertigo from the constant rush of water below me. Or look round, hoping to see the sight I knew I wouldn't—Nicholas speeding down the road in his Land Cruiser.

As I headed further and further out over the river and away from the support of the bank, I could feel the girders trembling underneath me. I told myself that they could not break and would surely not slip now, but even so, the sensation was terrifying and I found I was shaking, too. Memories I hadn't even known about came rushing back. A gray torrent streaming into the car. The pummeling noise on its roof as it was consumed by the river. Opening my mouth to scream and choking instead, with no air left, nothing to breathe, only a darkening flood.

I felt myself sway... I was going to fall. I clutched at the metal, breathing hard, sweat springing out on my skin. It took all my strength of will to find my balance and drag my gaze away from the hypnotic flow beneath.

"Help!" I yelled, but there was no answer, only the noise of the waters. Nobody to see me or save me this time... I was entirely alone. Frozen in place, there was no way I could turn around and go back. My limbs were aching and my hands burning with the effort of clutching the chilly steel. I knew if I stared down again, the raging floods would seem to inhale me, but when I looked ahead, the distance that I still had to cover appeared vast and impassable.

"One small step at a time, Erin," I whispered, my voice quivering. It took all my courage to let go of the girder with my right hand and grab it again a little further on.

"Now the left," I told myself, shaking a trickle of sweat out of my eyes. I focused on the couple of feet of steel in front of me and tried to shut everything else out of my world.

Left, right, left, right. Inch by painful inch I worked my way across the unsteady girders.

Finally, I made it, just as my shaking limbs were about to give out on me. I hauled myself into a painful crouch, then grabbed at the bank and scrambled up.

I dropped to my knees, my hands propped on my thighs, my head spinning. I was breathing hard and my hair was wet with sweat. But I had done it. I'd made it across. I was exhausted, filthy, muddied, and tangled, with rust stains on my palms and the knees of my jeans. But I had achieved my goal. I'd cut the ties. Leopard Rock, and its owner, were behind me forever.

A flash of Nicholas—where was he? I imagined him, his job done, his eyes shadowed with tiredness, enduring the long wait until his helicopter was ready and he could fly back to the estate.

I wondered how he'd feel when he found my note. Disappointed that I had left before he got back? Relieved there would be no awkward goodbyes?

I would never know. In any case, what was I doing thinking about Nicholas while I was waiting for my husband? It was time to take a leaf out of Nicholas's own book; to leave my past behind and think about my future. I stood up on wobbly legs and limped slowly up the steep dirt road.

✢ ✢ ✢

Vince arrived twenty minutes later, by which time I'd walked some way further and had managed to make myself a little more presentable by brushing some of the mud away and rubbing my hands over the dewy grass to help rinse off the stains.

He got out of the Land Rover and walked over to me. Despite the early morning hour, he was impeccably groomed, his black hair spiky with gel, a trace of carefully outlined designer stubble on his jaw, wearing stylish True Religion jeans and a charcoal-colored Armani T-shirt. He looked as immaculate, as handsome as he'd done on the day I met him at his photographic exhibition.

"Hello, babes." He kissed me briefly on the lips before stepping back and regarding me with his dark, smoldering gaze.

"Hey Vince." I smiled at him, but he didn't return the smile.

"You look like shit," he observed, and although his words were not said with any particular malice, I felt my own smile waver and then disappear. How I must look, to him? Tired eyes, tangled hair, no trace of make-up, muddied, and barefoot, with bleeding palms and stained and crumpled clothes.

"I know. I'm sorry," I said reflexively, and could have kicked myself for having fallen back into the routine of apologizing and placating him. Still, he was right. I didn't look my best, and that was a problem for Vince, who set great store by appearance.

Briefly, I thought about what I had become during the months I'd known my husband. Far better groomed. Aware of brand names and quality. Conscious of my image, and of the image I projected to others, particularly him.

We'd shared many serious, deep moments although, looking back on it, I could never remember Vince having made me smile as much, in our entire relationship, as Nicholas had in just a few days.

"I crawled over those girders back there. That's how I got here," I told him, pointing to the river behind me, hoping to lighten his mood or at least impress him. "Do you want to take a drive down to see them better?"

Vince glanced at the river, then back at me, and with a shrinking of my heart I could see the disbelief in his expression.

"Whatever," he said. "That road looks crappy. I don't want to get the car stuck. You're here with me now. That's what counts, hey, baby? We're together. Let's get back to Royal Africa. One of your bags was in my car, so there's some of your gear in the hotel room."

"Oh, that is good news." I climbed into the car and we set off.

I'd been worried about what I would say to Vince if he asked me about my stay at Leopard Rock, and what we would speak about if he didn't. I had dreaded trying to fill the silence between us. In the end I needn't have worried. He turned up the music in the Land Rover to a level that did not allow for conversation, and I spent the drive back to the hotel listening, with relief, to R&B while pretending to be asleep.

The five-star hotel where Vince was staying was the last word in opulence. It was decorated in ecru, wine red, and gold, with dark wooden ceilings, sweeping navy blue and forest green curtains. The walls were covered with drapes of African textiles and and safari-themed oil paintings. Sumptuous as it was, I would have swapped it in an instant for the light, bright, airy, and simple décor of Leopard Rock.

Stopping off at the front desk, self-conscious about walking through the glamorous lobby barefoot, I inquired whether any of my replacement credit cards had been delivered yet. The receptionist on duty said nothing had arrived yet, but that she would contact my room immediately if anything came in.

I followed Vince down the carpeted corridor and up a flight of stairs to our suite. I was beginning to feel nervous, as if I'd had a stay of execution that was now over. I knew that, soon, we would have to talk things through, and that he would question me in detail about what I had done while I was away from him. I needed to have answers prepared, and a story that would stand up to his interrogation.

"There's your bag," he said, when we were in the spacious bedroom.

The small leather carry case I'd never thought I would see again was resting on the ottoman. Oh, the relief of finding that it contained my make-up, my perfume, two pairs of shoes, and a few items of clothing that I'd thrown in at the last minute in case I needed anything extra to wear.

Vince sat down on one of the armchairs and began reading something on his iPhone. He was clearly not in a mood for conversation, so I went into the bathroom and spent the next hour showering, fixing up my nails, blow drying my hair to glossy perfection, and doing my make-up.

I couldn't help it. Nowhere were the memories of Nicholas more vivid than when I stood under the shower. The patter of the water brought to mind the rain that had been beating down on the thatched roof when I had first regained consciousness in the lodge. It reminded me of the swimming pool where I had lost myself in our first kiss; the waterfall where we had first made love.

It was there, under that running water, while I was washing the last trace of him, the last smell of him, off my skin, that I came to the realization that deep down I had known for a while.

I was going to have to tell Vince everything.

I could not go forward in our marriage carrying this lie with me. I had broken a contract of trust, and as painful as it might be, and even if it meant sacrificing our relationship, it was what my conscience was telling me to do.

The only question was—how and when to break the news?

I made myself up immaculately before changing into fresh clothes, including a black top I knew Vince liked. When I came out again, my hair shiny and groomed, my body fragrant, his nod of approval told me that I had redeemed myself in his eyes.

"I'm going to be busy now," Vince said. "I have to Photoshop all my images and send them through by the end of the day."

"Do you want some help?" I offered, but he shook his head. The rejection sent a pang through me. Vince had always accepted my help in the past.

"Before you start…" I began, gathering my courage together, but my incipient confession was interrupted by the ringing of the telephone by the bed.

Frowning, Vince got up and answered.

"Yes," he said. "Yes, she's here. She must come down to reception? For what?"

He waited, listened. "Okay." Replacing the phone, he turned to me. "I don't know exactly what they want. I can't understand the locals here when they try to speak English. Something's arrived for you, and they need you to sign a form, I think. Anyway, you must go down there now." He checked the time on his phone. "I'll see you at breakfast in ten minutes."

"I'll see you there," I said, and hurried out of the room, grateful that the inevitable showdown had at least been postponed.

Downstairs, I saw it was eight-thirty a.m. and a new receptionist was on shift.

"Mrs. Mitchell?" she smiled.

"That's me," I confirmed.

"I have this for you." She passed me a cream-colored envelope with the hotel logo on the front.

"Thank you," I said, taking the envelope and turning away, but her words stopped me.

"If you could open it here, please?"

"Okay. But why…?"

"I was told to make sure that you stay here while you read it, ma'am."

Instructions from the credit card company? I didn't understand at all. Frowning in confusion, I tore open the envelope.

Inside was not the Visa card I'd been expecting. Instead, I found a room card with the hotel's logo on it, and a folded compliments slip.

Opening the compliments slip, my eyes widened and my heart started to race.

There was a short, printed message on it.

This card is for room 101. Use it if you need it. N.

Nicholas?

Suddenly terrified that Vince had followed me down here, I glanced round, but there was no sign of him. I stood for what seemed like a long time, looking down at the page through eyes that were blurry with tears. I felt breathless with shock, ridiculously emotional at the fact I'd heard from Nicholas again.

He had already found out that I had left the lodge. How had he known so fast? Had Miriam told him that I had gone missing and he'd put two and two together? No, of course—he knew Hennie, the hotel owner. So perhaps, when Miriam had contacted him to tell him I was gone, Nicholas had phoned Hennie and found out I was here.

"We can hold the card for you here at the desk if you'd like to come by for it later," the receptionist said. "I've been instructed to tell you that you must use the room at any time you need to." Her voice was gentle.

I felt as touched, as protected by this gesture as if Nicholas had been there himself to put his arms around me to bid me farewell. When I first met him, I would never have thought of him as a gentleman, and yet, this gesture was one of pure chivalry. In spite of the fact I'd run away without even saying a proper goodbye, he'd been thoughtful enough to book me a private room—to be used, I supposed, to gather myself together if Vince and I ended up having a fight. Or to sleep, if Vince banished me from his bed.

I found myself smiling, and blinking tears away while I did.

"If you could please tell the sender thank you," I said, handing back the compliments slip. The card itself I put in my pocket. Room 101. Since ours was 214, I guessed 101 would be on the ground floor, in the opposite wing of the building.

Dabbing the tears carefully away from my eyes so as not to smudge my make-up, I made my way to breakfast to wait for Vince.

He didn't come.

I sat in the colorfully decorated dining room, watching other guests strolling to the buffet to pile their plates with tasty looking food, while the waiters kept my coffee cup and juice glass filled. I waited for half an hour, during which time I had two orange juices and two coffees.

Vince must have decided to skip breakfast, or order room service, I thought. Or perhaps something had come up—an important phone call from back home, or another project he needed to discuss. At any rate, having Vince not turn up after he'd said he would was not entirely unusual.

I returned to the bedroom. Knocked on the door.

No answer.

I went back downstairs and got a key card from the ever-helpful receptionist, and let myself in. Vince was not in the room and I could not see his phone anywhere, although his laptop was open on the desk, screensaver swirling. As I had thought, then, he'd had a call, probably while on his way to breakfast, and had gone somewhere private to take it.

I sat down at the desk to wait for him, and as I did so, my elbow brushed against the wireless mouse. The movement caused the screensaver to dissolve and the image that was open in Photoshop appeared in vivid detail.

My mouth fell open as I gazed at it.

It was a close-up artistic photograph of a woman's breast. It was bigger than mine, full, plump, and perfectly rounded in a way that made me think it might have been cosmetically enhanced. The skin was flawlessly pale, the nipple a deep pink in color, elongated and aroused and gleaming with moisture. It was pierced through its center by a small, bright golden ring.

The depth of field in the picture did not allow for me to see the background in sharp focus, but as I stared in shock from the photo to the hotel room and back again, I realized where it had been taken. Here, in this bedroom. I could see the place where the gold and maroon stripe of the wall hanging matched up with a horizontal line near the door-frame's upper corner that Vince had not yet Photoshopped out.

This must be Helena. Vince had told me about her pierced nipples, during a time soon after we'd started dating when he'd been half encouraging me and half bullying me to have mine done as well. My refusal to entertain the idea of having my nipples pierced, or my breasts augmented, which he had also suggested, had sent him into a sulk for a week.

Now, staring at this photo, I understood why Vince had not wanted any help with his editing. He hadn't only been doing the *Vogue* shoot. He had also been doing… this.

His artistic eye shone from the picture. Just as he had intended the onlooker to do, I found myself wondering, imagining, whether the moistened shine on that puckered nipple had been made by ice… or by saliva… or…

The click of the hotel room door opening made me jump.

CHAPTER 20

VINCE PUSHED THE DOOR open and strode angrily into the room.

"Where were you, Erin? I thought I asked you to join me at…"

He stopped speaking, abruptly, as he saw my face.

"You look pissed. What's your problem?"

"This is my problem," I told him icily.

I swiveled the laptop round to face him, and watched him go very still as he saw the image on its screen. He paused for only a moment before recovering himself. His voice loud and accusing, he demanded, "What the hell are you doing messing around with my computer?"

"I was in the dining room," I told him in a voice that sounded surprisingly calm and level. "You weren't. I came back here to wait for you and I bumped the mouse by mistake. You left this image open. I assume there are others, but I haven't looked."

Vince's chin jutted. "You should have waited for me at breakfast."

"What's breakfast got to do with this?" I asked, hurt and outrage quavering in my voice.

He shrugged. "What's work got to do with anything? I told you when we first started dating that I sometimes photograph nude models."

"Yes, but not ex-girlfriends."

"I had a job come in from *Playboy*. Very good money. They wanted an erotic shoot, but something different. Something classy. Helena was here already and she has the right size tits. Yours are too small, baby. Nobody reading *Playboy* wants to look at B-cups. And if you look at the other pics, she's also got a yummy tattoo near her…"

"I don't want to look at them!"

"Well, I told you this is how things are." Vince stared at me, managing to look both smug and aggressive. "If you don't like it, leave. The nearest hotel is about twenty miles away. See how far you get with no credit card or ID."

Listening to Vince, I felt helpless. Crushed by his words and the forcefulness of his attitude, I was ready to back down and agree with him when I suddenly found myself emboldened by a surge of anger.

"That's fine, actually," I said dismissively. "You can do what you want. Photograph what you like. I'm going to take you up on the offer of the trial separation you suggested on the phone. We need time apart. Things aren't working between us, Vince, and if you want an idea of how badly they're not working…"

His face was like thunder. I wished fervently I had thought before opening my big mouth. But it was too late for me to stop, so I pressed on.

"If you want an idea of how badly they're not working, I'll tell you. While you were prancing around in this hotel room photographing your ex-girlfriend's breasts, I was having an affair with the owner of the lodge where I was staying. I'm not proud of…"

I was going to tell him that I was not proud of my decision. That it had been foolish and stupid and entirely my own fault, and that I regretted it deeply. But I did not get a chance to say any of that, because before I could, he grabbed my wrist and yanked me up from my chair.

"You did what?" he yelled. His lips were curled back from his teeth and I could see the silvery gleam of the fillings in his molars, could smell strong coffee on his breath. His fingers dug viciously into my skin and I cried out, feeling cold with terror.

"Ow! Stop!"

I had forgotten how strong Vince was when he was trying to hurt me.

"No!" I pleaded, as his grip tightened.

"What do you mean, an affair? Are you fucking kidding me?"

He grabbed a fistful of my hair, tugged hard. I felt roots rip out of my head, a sharp, exquisite agony, blood storming through my veins. I was tempted—so tempted—to shout that I'd been lying to him, that I'd only been trying to provoke him with my words, but I knew it was too late for that, and that even if I did, I would still suffer the consequences of his fury.

Screaming was something I could do—if I yelled loud enough perhaps somebody would be alerted—but, anticipating my strategy, he clamped his hand over my mouth, crushing my lips against my teeth so hard I tasted blood.

I forced my jaws open and snapped them shut, managing to get the flesh of one of his fingers in between them. With a shout of pain he snatched his hand away.

I had just one chance, one moment left to act, and I needed to take it.

I lunged forward, yanking myself out from his grasp, feeling a raw fire in my scalp as more hairs pulled loose. I dived for the door and snatched it open and then I was out, running down the corridor as if my life depended on it, knowing that if I could find another person then I would be safe, because Vince would never lay a finger on me in public; only when we were alone.

He was pursuing me. I could hear the thudding of his footsteps. I hurtled down the stairs, my shoe catching on the edge of a rug and sending me flying. I sprawled onto the carpet, raw agony flaring in my injured palms. No time to think about how much it hurt. I was up again and on the move, my breath sobbing in my chest as I rounded a corner. Finally, thank God, there was a chambermaid approaching, her trolley loaded up with fresh linen. I sprinted past her knowing Vince would not; that he would drop back to a normal pace until he was out of her sight.

That bought me a few precious seconds of time.

What to do? Where to go? Was I going to throw myself at the mercy of the hotel receptionists, explaining what had happened and asking them to keep me safe until I could get out of here?

No guarantee, though, that Vince wouldn't smooth talk his way into persuading them that I was delusional.

There was only one place I could go now. I sprinted across the reception area and headed through to the opposite wing of the hotel. In room 101, which was all the way at the end of the passage, I could be safe.

I fumbled the key card into the slot, praying it would open without a problem, checking behind me as I did so, dreading that Vince would catch up with me. He would have slowed down to cross the lobby, though, and afterwards would not know which hallway I'd gone down—passages led to conference rooms, to the kitchen, a ladies' bathroom.

The door to room 101 clicked open and I burst inside, slamming it behind me.

Inside, air-conditioned quiet and tranquility. Blessed silence. I stumbled to the sofa and flung myself on the cushions, my legs suddenly boneless.

On the table in front of me I saw a small ice bucket and a clean hand towel had been set out. My eyes filled with tears as I realized exactly why Nicholas had thought to offer me this haven. Not just for my emotional well-being, but for my physical safety. He had lived with abuse as a child... he had guessed this would happen.

I soaked the towel in the ice and pressed it onto my burning scalp and throbbing lips, its cold touch offering instant relief. Blood feathered out across the white linen like a spreading flood. I shut my eyes and wept softly.

I knew it would be too dangerous to leave this room. I would stay here until my credit card arrived. Once I had that card, I would have my independence back—enough, at least, that I could arrange transportation and alternative accommodation while I waited for my temporary passport to be ready.

I dialed the front desk and asked the receptionist if she could please call me in this room when my card arrived, and that I did not want anybody else to know where I was.

"No problem, Mrs. Mitchell," she reassured me.

In spite of this, I started feeling fearful again. What if somebody, in all innocence, told Vince about this room? What if he managed to talk his way into obtaining an access card?

I spent a few minutes fretting over this possibility. In fact, I was considering whether I should drag some furniture in front of the door just in case, when I heard the sound I had dreaded—the click and whirr of the latch opening.

Shit, shit, a chambermaid would have knocked, so it had to be him. It had to. And I had nothing to defend myself but…

I picked up the ornamental wrought-iron bowl on the desk and hoisted it high above my head. When Vince came in, I was going to throw it at him, and then I was going to dive past him and…

The door swung wide and in walked Nicholas de Lanoy.

Nicholas stopped in his tracks when he saw me struggling to brandish the heavy bowl, and for a long moment we stared at each other. My heart thundered in my chest. The bowl slipped from my grasp and thudded down onto the table.

My lips felt numb, and not just from the ice I'd applied.

"You're hurt, Erin," he said softly. "Are you all right?"

"What are you doing here?" I asked. My voice trembled. I couldn't stop looking at him, noticing he was wearing a pair of jeans I hadn't seen before and a black Polo shirt. His gold-tanned skin, his broad shoulders, his sandy hair—all so familiar and dear, although the expression of deep concern in his pale eyes was new to me.

"I came to find you," he said.

He locked the door behind him and strode over to me.

Then I was in his arms, wrapped tightly around me, my eyes flooding. I held him close, unable to believe he was really here. I had been so sure I would never see him again. My deep, shaky breaths did not stop me from weeping in relief.

"You came to find me?"

"I had to make sure you were okay."

"I am," I told him. "Thanks to you."

"I was so worried." He touched my lips with a gentle fingertip.

"I told Vince about you. I might have done it in a more tactful way if I hadn't seen he'd been photographing his ex-girlfriend's breasts," I said.

"He did more than that," Nicholas said, his voice cold.

"Huh? What are you talking about? How do you know?" Scrubbing tears from my eyes, knowing it would be smudging my recently applied mascara but that Nicholas would not mind, I stared at him.

"Hennie told me a couple of days ago. He said your husband and some blonde were all over each other at dinner soon after she arrived, and they spent the night in the same bedroom. The chambermaid found evidence of cocaine use the next morning. Read into it what you want. I should have told you at the time, but I didn't. I worried it might only make things worse and drive a wedge between us. That you wouldn't have believed me—or that you would have chosen to believe his lies."

Soberly, I thought about it, wondering what I would in fact have done. I didn't know what the answer to that was. All I knew was that with every day that had gone by at Leopard Rock, I had ended up trusting Vince less and Nicholas more.

"When I found you had gone, I wished I'd told you. Wished I'd been able to change your mind, to stop you from choosing to run. Worst of all, I couldn't get to you immediately. I had to organize a hired car. Which I did as fast as I could."

"Well—thank you again." I didn't know what else to tell him. I feared that anything else I said might betray the depths of my feelings for him.

"Sit here with me. We need to talk." He guided me over to the bed and helped my trembling body gently down onto the cool smooth sheets. Then, with his arm around me, he continued in a serious voice.

"I didn't just come here to make sure you were safe, Erin. I wanted to ask you to come back with me."

"To come back with you? To Leopard Rock?" I could hear the incredulity in my own voice.

"Yes."

"But… for how long, Nicholas? Another week? Two? I don't think I can do that, because…" Oh, well. Time to be honest, whatever the cost. "Because I've fallen for you in a big way, and it was difficult enough leaving the first time."

"Is that why you ran?" His voice was gentle.

"Yes. That's why I ran."

He took a deep breath. "The timing couldn't have been worse. Because I was about to ask you to stay. And not for another week, or for another two."

I stared at him, my eyes wide with amazement. In my head, desire warred with disbelief. The prospect of returning to the lodge… staying there with him, without the inevitable prospect of a return flight looming ahead… but how was this possible? What had happened to the libertine who had made me such a brazen proposal less than a week ago?

"But… but we hardly know each other," I stammered out.

"That's why I want to spend a long time getting to know you better," Nicholas said, his voice gentle. "A very long time. I'm thinking years, although it may well take decades. Or the remainder of the century, if you'll have me. I'm totally sure about what I want, Erin. But if you're unsure, we can take it a week at a time. In which case, I'd like to invite you to come back and spend just one more week with me."

I found myself blinking tears out of my eyes again as new emotions rushed in. Joy… relief… hope. I had not allowed myself to entertain any of them—had never thought they would be possible. I had never been able to imagine a future with Nicholas. Now, it felt as if the foundations of my world had been rocked. Instead of leaving alone for the plane back to New York, I could be returning to the estate, to be with the man who, in just a few short days, had managed to turn my life around—and had captured my heart.

"I was planning to ask you to stay," he said. "I was doing my best to gather my courage together, but it wasn't easy, not with your situation as it was—and given how much your decision meant to me. Then you pre-empted me by leaving, and I thought I had lost you.

Worse, I thought I'd allowed you to go back to a situation where you could be hurt."

"Are you sure…" Suspicion surfaced briefly. It was a question I had to ask.

"What?"

"Are you sure you are not just inviting me back because you're trying to protect me from an abusive husband?"

"No, Erin. I'm inviting you back because I am totally and utterly smitten with you. Because I'm in love with you."

"You're what?" was all I could get out. My heart was racing. *Was this really happening? Had he truly said these words?*

"I'm in love with you," he repeated. "In the time that you've been in my life, you've changed it for the better. You've helped me understand that I am not the same person I was ten years ago, and that I'd only be fooling myself if I carried on trying to behave that way. When I realized you'd left, it felt as if my world had ended. I don't know if you feel the same way, but I can only hope that you do. Or that you are prepared to give us a chance, even if it means walking away from your marriage."

"I am," I said, finding my voice at last. "And I feel the same way about you, Nicholas—my brain is just a little scrambled at the moment because I've spent the best part of the last week feeling everything you've been telling me now, and trying to deny it all. I've been dreading that damned bridge being rebuilt, more than you'll ever know."

I turned to face him, glowering up at him in mock anger. "And I've been dreading getting the brush-off from Mr. de Lanoy, just like every other married woman he's entertained at his estate."

"From the moment you opened your eyes and held my hand, that wasn't going to happen," Nicholas explained. "Even on that first night when we watched the stars together, I was trying to convince myself as much as you that it would be possible to let you go so easily. A day or two later, I knew that was never going to happen; that I'd found the person I wanted to spend my life with. I might have saved you from drowning, Erin, but in an equally important way, you've rescued me, too."

My jaw dropped at the words. Oh, God, this was real—this was something that surely had a chance of working. And didn't everyone deserve a chance at happiness?

For a moment I saw my two futures, divergent paths stretching out in front of me.

In one, I returned to New York, moved out of Vince's loft, went off on my own again. Most probably I'd end up going back to my nomadic lifestyle. A few months here, a few months there. Always roaming, traveling, moving on—although what I was running from, or searching for, I could never truly explain.

And in the other, I went with Nicholas... to a life that would be filled with love. Who knew exactly where that decision would take me, where in the future or in the world we would end up traveling, what we would do... but we would be together. I would be with a man who complemented and completed me, who made me feel, through his presence, as if half of me had until now been missing.

"So," he said. "Shall we go?"

"My bag!" The carry on satchel containing the only personal possessions I had in the country was in the hotel room where I guessed, even now, Vince would be pacing the carpet and smoldering.

"Do you want me to go and get it?"

The message was clear. I was not to risk being alone with my husband again. I knew that if I asked for the bag Nicholas would willingly go up to the bedroom and get it for me—and I had no doubt who would come out the victor, should there end up being a physical confrontation between the two men.

But what was I leaving behind, really? A few clothes and cosmetics—items I had managed perfectly well without.

"There are some good shops in Nelspruit," Nicholas said, as if reading my mind. "We can make a stop before we pick up the helicopter, and buy whatever you need. There's an excellent camera store there as well."

"Well, then," I told him. Exuberance filled me. I stood up, grasped his hands, and pulled him to his feet and into my arms. "We'd better get going. Among other activities, I have a lot of photography to catch up on."

EPILOGUE

A YEAR HAD GONE by since I had returned to Leopard Rock.

Now I climbed out of the yellow cab, hearing the background buzz of voices, traffic, horns. Shivering, I wrapped my trench coat tightly around me and angled my umbrella so that it offered my hair some protection from the chilly blowing rain that had turned the afternoon cold and gloomy.

New York City in November… a world away from the South African sunshine I had left behind—not recently, but months ago.

As I hurried along the paved sidewalk, my thoughts returned to my first meeting with Nicholas—to the moment when I'd opened my eyes in darkness and heard his voice, felt the touch of his hand.

Brent, the doorman, pulled open the glass door that led into the marble-tiled lobby of the apartment building where I had lived with Vince. Stepping inside, I found my mind filled with thoughts that were as dark as the weather.

I couldn't help remembering the man I thought I had loved, and who had told me he had loved me. I thought sadly of loss, of shattered dreams, of a future that had looked golden and had, so swiftly, turned sour.

"Mrs. Mitchell?" Brent said with some surprise as I reached into my pocket and took out a small padded envelope.

Shaking the water off my umbrella, I smiled.

"I've been divorced since January," I told the doorman. "I'm not Mrs. Mitchell anymore. I came by to return a few valuables."

"Would you like to take them up to the apartment? Mr. Mitchell is away this week, but he did advise me you'd be round. I'll come with you if you don't mind."

"Thanks. I'll only be a minute. There are personal items I'm supposed to collect as well."

Brent and I walked over to the elevator, and he pressed the button for the sixteenth floor, where Vince and I had lived.

Our divorce, although messy, had been conducted entirely through our lawyers. Not once had Vince or I spoken, or met face to face. I'd already been informed he would be out of town when I arrived, but I hadn't thought he'd refuse to let me into his apartment without the doorman supervising me.

When Brent tapped on the door, I understood why.

After a short pause, it was opened, and I stared in surprise at the woman in the doorway.

Tall, slender, vulnerable-looking, she was wearing heavy make-up. Her shiny brown hair was perfectly styled and she was fashionably dressed in white jeans, high-heeled Burberry boots, and a Chanel blouse.

Brent cleared his throat. "Good morning, ma'am. We've come to drop off this envelope. Mr. Mitchell knows about it."

"Yes, he did tell me," she said, glancing at me warily. "Come in."

She stepped aside. It was only as I walked into the apartment that I noticed the single flaw in her perfection.

Her right hand was heavily bandaged; the wrist encased in a stabilizing support splint. When I saw that, and the dark bruises above her elbow, I went cold all over. Gooseflesh prickled my spine.

Brent handed the envelope to her and she took it in her left hand, then placed it on the table in the hallway. Beyond, I saw the apartment was exactly as I remembered it. Modern, soulless, immaculate. It was as if I'd last seen it a day ago. Nothing had changed.

"There should be something for Mrs. Mitchell to collect," Brent said.

"I'm sorry," she said, turning to me and speaking the words as if they were rehearsed. "Vince said to tell you he threw away the items you were asking about. Your photographic portfolio, and the old portrait of you and your brother."

Rage welled up inside me. My portfolio represented my life's work… and that picture was the last one that had been taken of Aidan and me before he died. A coward to the last, Vince hadn't even had the courage to tell me himself. I wanted to scream out my anger at this woman—I drew a sharp breath to do so, and then let it silently out again.

All I could do was let go, move on, put this last vicious act of revenge behind me. His new girlfriend needed my sympathy, not my rage.

With a huge effort, I controlled my feelings.

"It's not important," I told her. "What's your name?"

"Hayley," she said.

"I'm Erin. I was married to Vince, as I'm sure you know. In the envelope are the rings he gave me. An engagement ring and a wedding ring." I looked at her wrist again before adding, "They're valuable items of jewelry, but they weren't worth the hurt."

Hayley's face twisted and she looked away, fixing her gaze on the polished tiles.

"There are numbers you can call for counseling," I told her gently. "Places you can stay if you decide to leave him. Nobody should have to put up with abuse. You can contact me if you need any help."

I handed her one of my new business cards with my international contact details and email address.

She was still staring down at it when Brent closed the door behind her.

Back in the lobby, I hurried to the exit, opened my umbrella, and stepped out into the rain again.

He was waiting for me, right there outside the building, his coat collar turned up, his dark golden hair now plastered wetly around his face.

My heart leaped, as it always did when I saw him—even when we had been parted for only a few minutes.

"Nicholas de Lanoy," I told him sternly, hurrying over to him with the umbrella. "I thought I told you to stay in the cab."

He grinned unrepentantly, slid an arm around me, kissed me hard.

"When do I ever do what I'm told?"

"Um—well, from time to time you do, actually. It always surprises me."

"Not this time. I thought I'd better wait nearby, just in case."

"It's okay. Vince wasn't there."

"And your belongings? Did you get them back?"

I shook my head. "I didn't. But it doesn't matter. I can put together a new portfolio. And Aidan's memory will always be in my heart."

Nicholas nodded solemnly, then enfolded me in a tight embrace.

Nicholas and I had been together for one happy, incredible year so far. Much of it had been spent at Leopard Rock, and we'd been surprisingly busy. As well as the day-to-day running of the estate and my photography, there had been business opportunities to be managed and explored, and charitable ventures to be undertaken, including opening a new school in the nearby village. And the high point of the year had been our wedding in May—a beautiful ceremony held at the estate and attended by all our friends and family.

We'd taken an extended holiday in late August and had traveled through the States together. We'd stopped off in Florida to visit my mother, in San Francisco where my father now lived, and most recently, we'd spent ten days in New Jersey, having a wonderful time with Sam and Mike and Jen.

New York City was our next to last stop. After this, we'd decided on the spur of the moment to fly up to Canada, where heavy early winter snowfalls at Lake Louise were currently creating perfect conditions for great skiing.

We walked briskly back towards the waiting cab.

"So Vince really was out of town for the week?" Nicholas asked.

"Surprising, isn't it?" I said, picking up the humor in his voice.

"You'd have thought he would have stayed here, what with that photo exhibition opening tonight. A really hotshot new photographer, I hear, and incredibly sexy, too. What's her name again…?"

Laughing, I dug my fingers into the ticklish spot on his side that I'd been delighted to discover. "Her name is Erin de Lanoy. And the work being shown at the exhibition was taken in South Africa. The collection is entitled, 'After the Floods.'"

"Ah, yes." Nicholas nodded. "I'm looking forward to it. In fact, we should probably head back to the hotel now to get ready. Four Seasons, please," he told the driver, as we climbed into the cab.

"We don't have to get ready just yet," I told him, checking my watch. "We've got two and a half hours before we have to leave."

"That's good," His pale eyes gleamed, and as his hand caressed my thigh I forgot how cold I'd been just a minute ago. "Because, luckily, I've just thought of a way to pass the time that I know you're going to enjoy."

ABOUT
THE AUTHOR

JASSY DE JONG was inspired to write her first novel, *Random Violence*, after getting hijacked at gunpoint in her own driveway. She has written several other thrillers, including *Stolen Lives, The Fallen*, and *Pale Horses*. Having traveled widely around the world, she lives today in the northern suburbs of Johannesburg with her partner Dion, two horses, and two cats.

Photo credit:
Conrad de Jong

Acknowledgments

Writers, like romantic heroines, need a perfect partner. I am fortunate enough to have several, all of whom have earned my deepest thanks.

To Dion, the love of my life and the first person to read every word I write, I am grateful beyond words for your enthusiasm, humor, and loving support.

Thanks to my incredible agent Stephany Evans from FinePrint Literary Management for all the great work you have done on my behalf.

Thanks to Robert Astle, Jillian Ports, and the Astor + Blue Editions editorial team for your wonderful enthusiasm for the story and for the eagle-eyed edits and polishing.

A final thank-you to my younger sister, Sophie Ranald, for your encouraging comments on the first draft, and the reminder that Americans don't eat Marmite!